Enormous, renegade cows were roaming around Clem's ranch, trampling the land, hiding in crevasses, growing healthier, heavier and more territorial with each passing day. Clem had kicked herself a thousand times for not dong better research before buying the cows. Not that it mattered. She was stuck with them now. She'd had five freelance outfits look at the cows. Each and every one had refused to take on the job of rounding them up. Finally she begged the last outfit for a name. There had to be someone who could help her.

The cowboys exchanged glances. One shrugged and another kicked at the dust. Then a third said, "Ma'am, just take your losses and get a real job."

Clem could have laughed at the irony. This was the only job she was qualified for. She glared at them. "Tell me who can help me."

The tall one eventually said, "Can't vouch for him. He and his partners did some jail time. Even if you could find him, he won't help."

"Why not?" Clem's voice was curt.

"Retired."

"Give me his name," she'd begged. She wasn't going to let an itty-bitty complication like retirement get in her way.

With a sigh, the cowboy told her. "Dexter Scott. Trust me, ma'am. You'd be better off if you didn't find him."

He was probably right, but Clem had two choices—work with Dexter Scott or lose her family's ranch.

Dear Reader,

When starting this book, I was plagued by doubts. After all, what would a suburban girl like me know about cowboys and feral cows? However, as I searched the deeper recesses of my mind, I realized that during the late seventies while I was swallowing ten to fifteen Harlequin novels a week, I was also drinking generous doses of good old-fashioned Westerns.

It was not the guns or the intrigues that drew me to those rough-and-tumble books of the West, but the lonely, isolated men who were so often reluctant heroes. In my mind, I always added a heroine for the hero, the one person who could unlock the gates to a cowboy's heart and soul.

Dexter Scott is a man with many gates, some locked, some not. But they all serve the same purpose—self-protection. When Clementine Wells manages to get through every gate he has, Dexter realizes that love eliminates the need for gates.

Please join my recalcitrant hero and determined heroine as they discover that independence is not a good reason to miss out on love. And that sometimes, there's greater independence in a loving relationship and only pressing loneliness without it.

Sincerely,

Susan Floyd

P.S. I love to hear from my readers. You can reach me at: P.O. Box 2883, Los Banos, CA 93635 or via e-mail on my author's page at www.superauthors.com.

Books by Susan Floyd

HARLEQUIN SUPERROMANCE

890—ONE OF THE FAMILY
919—MR. ELLIOTT FINDS A FAMILY
987—FAITH AND OUR FATHER

A Cowboy for Clementine

Susan Floyd

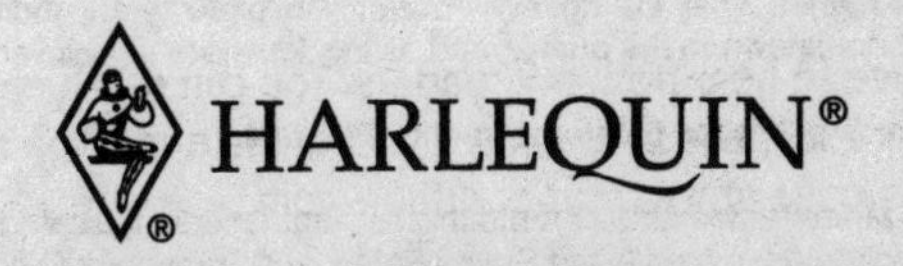

TORONTO • NEW YORK • LONDON
AMSTERDAM • PARIS • SYDNEY • HAMBURG
STOCKHOLM • ATHENS • TOKYO • MILAN • MADRID
PRAGUE • WARSAW • BUDAPEST • AUCKLAND

ISBN 0-373-71029-1

A COWBOY FOR CLEMENTINE

This edition published by arrangement with Harlequin Books S.A.

Visit us at www.eHarlequin.com

Printed in U.S.A.

I want to express my deep appreciation
to the entire Menefee family.
Colleen and Jerry, your generosity made this book
what it is. Scott and Chu'an (and little Kate, in utero)
thank you for the evening of feral cow viewing
and my first taste of venison jerky.
Jacob, may your Shuckabur live on always.

And special thanks to Anne and Jack Newins,
facilitators extraordinaire (even though I couldn't
make the hero Ishmael).

This book is dedicated to my mother,
June Ishimatsu Kimoto
who in the last year has proven to be one of
the most courageous women I know. Thank you, Mom.

PROLOGUE

Los Banos, California, late January

CLEMENTINE WELLS STOPPED her horse, Archie, on a steep slope and stared straight ahead, trying to peer through the brush that covered most of the pastureland on her family's 16,000-acre ranch. She thought she was mistaken, that she was seeing some kind of mirage.

She had known that she'd been duped, known that the man who'd sold her all the calves at a greatly reduced price saw *inexperience* tattooed across her forehead. She'd felt like a monster, branding those little calves with just nubbins of horns on their heads. Nothing big enough to even trim. Some of them had looked as if they'd been snatched from their mothers a mite too soon. She'd worried all through November she'd been sold runts that would be devoured by the cougars or would die in the cold. So she'd spent much of her time watching them, riding up to check on their progress and their growth. When her parents had come for Christmas, her father'd been impressed. He'd clasped his big hand on her shoulder and squeezed, telling her she'd done a good job, and she'd basked in the glow of his praise.

Her parents had left two days ago, and she'd ridden into the mountains today to check again. At first, her fears had seemed confirmed. The cows weren't where they were supposed to be at this time of year. She'd trailed endless paths hoping that at least a few had survived the December storms that usually brought them in closer to the ranch. Now, as she spotted the cow she and her dogs had spent the past half hour tracking, she realized she'd been worried for nothing.

The cow had taken them on quite a trek, and, with a surge of triumph, Clem saw that it had led her to a shallow valley where there were others, the Wells family brand prominent on their rumps. Clem smiled with relief. These cows weren't lost or dead. And the growth of these runts was very encouraging. It looked as if the joke was on the man who'd sold her the calves so cheaply. Why, if they continued to graze and grow at the rate they were, they'd be close to eight hundred pounds by April.

Elation ran through her and Clem allowed herself to smile. Her mother had been right. She was capable. Being taken care of first by her father and then her ex-husband hadn't ruined her for life. She was able to stand on her own feet, admittedly with some help. But this was *her* herd, these were *her* cows. Finally, she'd done something in her thirty-two years of living that would actually pay off.

Archie whinnied and Clem looked around to see she wasn't the only thing following the cow. Behind her was another one, wearing her brand, staring at her. Clem felt a little uneasy. Cows were prey animals. They wouldn't venture so close. In fact, as a rule, they skittered away when something threatening approached.

This cow appeared neither threatened nor skittish. Instead, it shook its head before lowering it and pointing its horns at Clem.

Impossible. Clem thought with a laugh. *Cows weren't aggressive, though this one sure looked like—*

The cow charged.

Archie stepped backward, and with her voice stuck in her throat and her heart pounding in her ears, Clementine Wells did what all good cowboys did in such a situation.

She ran.

She wheeled Archie out of the way and let him go, calling to her dogs at the same time. She could hear the sound of hooves pounding behind her, but was too afraid to look. Suddenly, Clem realized that for months she'd been worried about the wrong thing. Her cows were thriving in the Diablo mountain range. In the spring they'd be worth hundreds of thousands of dollars. But cows only made money after they were rounded up and brought to market.

At the best of times, with the gentlest of cows, roundups were hard. These cows were feral, getting them out of the mountains was going to be a nightmare.

CHAPTER ONE

Somewhere northeast of Barstow, California

KEEP OUT. Trespassers Will Be Shot.

Clementine Wells stared at the sign on the twenty-foot barbed-wire tension gate, and craned her neck, looking for any sign of a house, any sign of someone about to shoot her. This was where she'd find the one man who could help her? She was tempted to just turn around, drive the ten hours back home and call her father to tell him he was right. She had no business trying to be a rancher. It was mid-September, and she still hadn't been able to round up her herd.

She climbed back into the truck, shoved it into reverse, then stopped, fighting the fatigue of driving. She could see her mother as she'd looked more than a year ago.

"You can do it, Clementine."

"I don't know, Mom," Clem had hedged. "It's different running a ranch than working on it. I haven't done this kind of physical labor since… since before I went to college."

Before I married Nick went unsaid. Her mother hadn't approved of the marriage, hadn't approved of the fact that Clem had quit college in her junior year to follow Nick to San Jose, where they'd become wealthy overnight, riding the early dot.com wave. Until the divorce last year, Clem had not worked a full-time job in her entire adult life.

"Your father is a good man," her mother had told her. "But he's done too much for you. You need to know you can stand on your own two feet. Without us."

"But the ranch?" Clem had never even envisioned herself taking over the ranch. "I'm not sure I'd even know where to start."

"You've done every chore this ranch requires. You have a good mind. City people buy ranches all the time. Besides, if your father doesn't take to retirement, we can come back, if you're here."

Claire Wells made it seem so simple.

Jim Wells, however, wasn't as enthusiastic.

"The ranching business has changed, sweetheart," her father had said as they rode out to watch the sunset. "I'm not sure you're up to it. It's not the world you knew growing up."

Until that moment, Clem hadn't thought she was up to it, either, but the doubt and concern in her father's voice made her stop Archie.

"Not that I think you can't do it," Jim Wells had added, staring straight ahead.

"Mom thinks I can." Clem hadn't wanted her voice to sound so unsure. She'd realized at that moment, she wanted her father to think she could do it, too. "I can always call you for advice."

Her father had been silent, then cleared his throat and said, "Your mother has always wanted you to be independent."

"And now that I am?" She hadn't felt independent. Ask her to arrange a dinner party for ten and she could do it. Ask her what she wanted to do with the rest of her life and she felt as uncertain as she had when she was nineteen.

"You know, honey, you can always come to Arizona with us, just until you figure out what you want to do with your life. The new house has an extra bedroom."

Clem had swallowed. That would be even more humiliating. "If I ran the ranch for the next year or so, you could always come back if you find that retirement doesn't agree with you."

Her father started walking his horse again. "Honey, for the record, I don't think there is such a thing as going back. It's all about moving forward."

It's all about moving forward. Clementine got back out of the truck and studied the sign again, trying to make up her mind. She was the kind of person who obeyed signs. If a sign on a rest room door read Employees Only, she wouldn't go through it, even if she'd just had a Big Gulp. She'd walk all the way around the mall to find a public rest room.

The man behind that fence was the only person

who could protect her parents' retirement. She'd spent a good portion of their money and her own, and now she didn't think even her father could do *anything* that would solve this problem. It had grown—for lack of a better term—larger than even he could handle.

Ignoring the sign, she stuck out a tentative hand and rattled the gate. Yep. It was tight. She leaned over to the side to see what kind of latch it had. Just a rusty nail soldered to the chain. With gentle fingers, she tugged on the nail. It stuck. She tugged a little harder. Then it slid out and the gate sagged to the ground. She couldn't even see the warning that trespassers would be shot anymore. She stepped over the gate and waited for a maniac to charge her with a shotgun. But nothing happened. There was just the stillness of the desert, the unending road in front of her.

Dexter Scott might be a recluse, but she didn't believe he was a maniac. She'd done a lot of research on the man, searching for him ever since she'd heard his name. He'd been in jail for a couple of barroom fights, but there'd been nothing about him shooting defenseless women. She dragged the gate to the side of the road and, with a deep breath, got back in her truck and drove through.

It didn't take her long to figure out how to put the gate back up. So with the rusty nail in place, Clem drove on, aware of the peaceful red desert that surrounded her. The way she figured it, if she came upon a gate she didn't know how to unlatch, she'd take that as a sign and turn right around. But each gate, though different, was workable. As she drove past her fourth gate, she understood for the first time why the heroines in Alfred Hitchcock movies always looked in the closet.

Feeling bolder, Clementine inspected the last gate. This one was padlocked. She could justify opening gates that weren't locked, but even if she had the skills to pick locks, she wasn't sure she could ignore this sign. It'd be easy enough to turn around. No one had even detected her presence.

But she could see a tiny speck of a house maybe a mile in the distance. So close and yet so far. She leaned against the gate, solidly built out of steel slats, and considered her options. She could go home to the same problem that she hadn't been able to solve or she could be brave and ask this man to help her. She put her foot in one slat. She looked around. This gate would be easy enough to scale. She could walk that mile to the house. If anything, being on foot would make her appear less threatening. With a deep breath, she buttoned up her jeans jacket and started to climb. If Dexter Scott asked, she'd say she ran out of gas. Maybe he'd give her a ride back to the truck and then she'd be able to make her request.

As she straddled the top of the fence, she stopped and listened. What was that sound? Hoofbeats? Panic overwhelmed her, as she swung her trailing leg over and tried to get her balance. No doubt about it, those were hoofbeats behind her—right behind her. She could hear a horse snort. She froze. She was in the middle of nowhere and she was going to be shot. He could bury her body anywhere and no one would ever find her.

But she didn't hear a "Halt, who goes there," or anything else, just the panting of a horse. She didn't dare look over her shoulder, too chicken to stare down the barrel of a twelve-gauge shotgun. So this was how it ended. She decided that she wanted to die on the ground. Back still toward the rider, she jumped down.

When the rider didn't speak, Clem held up her arms to show she was unarmed. She swallowed hard and blurted over her shoulder, "I know I'm not supposed to be here, but I really need your help."

No answer, just the agitated prancing of hooves.

"I'm harmless, really. Just let me explain." Her mind was churning. Every fifteen minutes during her long drive it had occurred to her that there was no good reason in the world that this cowboy, this complete stranger would help her. But always, she'd gone forward.

With her breath held, Clementine willed her body into a slow rotation. At least she should see the face of the man who was going to shoot her, look in his eyes and appear brave. She backed up a step, bumping into the gate behind her.

Then she laughed, mostly with relief and a little hysteria.

"Well, well, well," Clem said, addressing the

beautiful brown horse. ''Where did you come from?''

The she looked at the empty saddle on the horse's back and asked, ''And where is your rider?''

SPITTING DUST. The only thing Dexter Scott hated worse than spitting dust was walking, and thanks to his newest horse, he was doing just that. He searched for the gelding. Tall, ornery, milk-chocolate with a white star between his eyes. There was nothing fitting that description within sight. Dex slapped the seat of his jeans, ignoring the billow of fine, red desert dirt, then slowly tested his shoulder. Pain shot through his rotator cuff, but he continued to flex the joint. The stabbing subsided slightly, which meant it wasn't dislocated again.

Thank God for that.

Spitting dust and walking was bad enough; another dislocation would turn the beautiful morning into a darn right ugly day. Now, where the hell was his hat? His eyes looked for it. And where the hell were Randy and Ryan? They said they'd be right behind him.

More than likely, they'd gone right back to their bunks. It was their off season. The Miller twins had just come off a torturous three-month chase that had taken its toll. Last night, as they sat in the living room of the old Victorian that Dexter's Uncle Grubb had left him and his sister, Joanna, telling him stories about the job, Dexter couldn't tell whether or not he missed the life. Ten years of chasing cows had been enough. Still, he'd had to fight down the twinges of envy as Randy and Ryan had embellished their exploits.

Five years ago, he'd have been right in the mix, they'd *all* been in the mix—Joanna, Randy, Ryan, Ben and Jody Thorton and their son, Mike. But nothing stayed the same. Nothing. Joanna was dead. Ben and Jody had gotten a divorce after Jody'd taken Mike and moved out. Ben had quit the life, just so he could have a shot at joint custody. Randy and Ryan had moved on to other jobs. And Dexter had just stayed put. The days after they'd buried Joanna had somehow slipped into months, months into years. He hadn't realized what a hermit he'd become until Randy's flamingo-pink truck had rattled down his deserted road, dust blowing behind the rear tires.

Dexter had spent most of the past three years building up a stable of horses, training them to track and hold wild cows. Part of his success had come from his ability to buy low and sell high. He spent a lot of time scouring the western states, looking for good stock considered "unsalvageable," ruined by inexperience or plain abuse. To Dexter Scott, no horse was unsalvageable.

Take for example this new horse. He'd driven to Nevada to purchase him after getting a tip off the Internet. Even neglected and underweight, this horse had been magnificent—energetic, alive in ways Dexter would never be again. The horse held promise, perfect for a cowboy who needed a good work horse and who understood the symbiotic relationship between man and beast—if, of course, the horse ever learned to accept a rider for any length of time.

Dexter frowned as he swiveled his arm again, trying to keep it from stiffening up. New Horse, as Randy referred to him, had shown a lot of progress in the past two months. He'd gained weight, and his dull coat was starting to turn glossy. He'd actually nickered in greeting when Dex had arrived this morning, politely accepting the carrot chunk he'd offered. This had prompted Dexter to saddle him up. When the horse carried the saddle in circles around the corral, following Dexter wherever he went, Dexter took this as a good sign. The next step was to get on. And surprise of surprise, New Horse allowed that and even responded properly to the pressure applied to his ribs. Dexter was feeling pretty good about his student as a glorious dawn broke over the desert.

But once out of the safety of the corral, with miles of dry foothills around him, New Horse got a big fat F in deportment. Dex spat out some gravel-like chunks and then ran his tongue over his teeth, hoping that wasn't actually a filling or worse, part of a tooth. He hated dental work more than he hated walking. His jaw ached, but he supposed that was because New Horse had just sent him tumbling head over ass.

Damn. The desert was still. Dex found himself a

rock and sat on it as his tongue continued its exploration around his teeth, carefully probing for any sharp, stabbing pain. So far, his teeth were the only intact parts of his body. He rubbed the bridge of his nose. It'd been broken more times than he could remember. His ribs had been cracked an equal number of times, his leg broken in two places twice. Fractured bones were part of the job description. But this was the first tumble he'd taken since before Joanna's accid—since before he'd retired.

Dexter shook off the onslaught of feelings that he hadn't invited and didn't want to stay. He thought instead of the Miller brothers, who were a party in and of themselves. They radiated fun and irreverence—Randy, the elder brother by four and a half minutes, especially.

Randy's heart was as big as his voice. Dexter still could hear Ryan's laughter last night as he defended himself from Randy's mock attacks with his malletlike fists. How long had it been since they'd all laughed like that? Afterward Randy had brought out his sketches. He suffered—although he would never use that word—from a rare form of color blindness, causing him to see the world in shades of gray. It was that very disability that made him so effective when chasing cows, because he looked for movement and shape, not color.

The color blindness also enabled him to produce the most compelling western art Dexter had ever seen. Randy could bench-press three hundred pounds, but then sketch in pen and ink the most delicate, heartrending portraits of cowboy life. Even though his artwork supported his lifestyle, Randy considered himself a dabbler, not an artist.

The sketches had made Dexter miss the life. They made him think there was much more to living than this desert. He stared in the direction of the main house. It was a heck of a long walk back. Up the small brown hills that obscured his vision of the ranch and down through the pass. Not a bit of water to be found. He flexed his shoulders, trying to ignore the pain that stabbed at his collarbone.

He gazed down at the brown dust on his boots, the heels worn down as were his spurs. They'd been silver at one time, but now had the dull look of well-used stainless steel. Suddenly, familiar hoofbeats made him perk up. New Horse had come to his senses and returned! Dex watched the distant cloud of dust advance. He knew that the horse had it in him. With training New Horse would become one of his best—

Who the hell was riding him?

The fine hairs on the back of his neck prickled as Dex watched the horse that threw him not an hour ago approach, the legs of his rider dangling on either sides. The brown horse remained steady in his trot, his mane glittering in the sunlight, unperturbed by the flapping stirrups.

Dexter swallowed hard.

This rider rode well, the skill apparent as New Horse slid down some crumbling red slate. How many times had he seen Joanna ride and skid only to recover and laugh at what she called a "cheap thrill"? The rider held herself in the same way, had the same tilt of the head. Impossible. He'd watched Randy pull Joanna's lifeless body out from under her horse. He'd touched her ice-cold hand.

The rider slowed so they wouldn't spray Dexter with dust and gravel. Dexter squinted up, from his rock unwilling to look into the face of the rider, unwilling to take the chance that it might be Joanna.

"Hey" was the best greeting he could muster.

"Lost your hat?" the rider asked, her voice clear and feminine.

"I THINK THIS IS YOURS." Clementine Wells offered the cowboy the sweat-stained gray hat she'd picked up along the trail. When she'd seen the empty saddle, she'd known there was either an angry or a dead cowboy out there somewhere. It was okay if he was angry, but it would do her no good if the man she'd spent more than a month searching for had managed to kill himself before he could help her.

So she had mounted the brown horse and followed the horse's tracks. When she'd found the hat, she'd felt a little better. She'd have something to give him. Two things. His horse and his hat. Surely, he would help her. Now she held out the hat even farther. His long arm reached up and he grimaced as his tanned fingers curled around the worn felt. He settled it on his head and looked significantly better.

Clem peered down and doubt flooded through her. If this was Dexter Scott, he was dusty and younger than she'd thought he'd be. Too young for retirement, too young to be as good as the grapevine said he was. Dark eyebrows arched up, framing hazel eyes that were as clear as a still lake at sunrise. Those eyes weren't dusty at all. And Clementine found herself staring into them, as if she were staring into the lake, watching flecks of gold sparkle along the water's edge.

Even though she had a feeling she was talking to him, she shifted in the saddle and said, "I'm looking for Dexter Scott."

"How'd you get in here?" His voice was gravelly, as if he hadn't spoken in a very long time. The horse she was riding skittered from side to side, and the cowboy stilled the horse by tugging the reins out of her hands. He did look menacing, his eyebrows coming together in a scowl, his mouth tight.

"Are you Dexter Scott?"

"How did you get in?" Each word was marked by a short staccato. He muffled a groan as he stood up.

"On the road." Clem repeated. She hated that he had the reins. It made her feel as if she was being held. And she was, by his eyes, by his angry stance.

He didn't say anything for a long time, his eyes flicking over her, running a lie detector test. Then he shook his head. "Gates are locked."

Nerves made her laugh. "Not if you know how to get through or climb over."

"You shut them?"

Clem bristled. Even she knew not to leave gates open. "Of course."

"I could shoot you, you know. Didn't you read the sign?"

"You could," Clem agreed, but patted the shotgun on the saddle in front of her. "If you had your horse, which you don't. It seems as if I do."

It occurred to Clem she shouldn't antagonize this man, so she fished out a tattered brochure from her back pocket and proceeded to read.

"This says you're an elite cowboy. A *cowboy's* cowboy," she said for emphasis. She stared at him doubtfully. He appeared anything but elite. Knowing that he'd fallen off his horse didn't give any credence to the brochure.

"Not anymore." He rubbed the nose of the horse, and moved to stand right next to her leg. "Retired."

God, he was tall. No wonder the stirrups hung so low. Clem refused to be put off by the definitive bleakness in his voice. She had more than six hundred feral cows roaming around on her father's ranch. Laboring all through spring and most of the summer, Clem and a crew of six transient cowboys had tried to round them up. *Tried* was the operative word. Oh, everyone had theories as to why the cows were so hard to catch. Difficult breed. Large size. Formidable horn growth. She had hoped that when the feed in the hills had dried up in the summer heat, these cows would want to come down and graze on her green pastures, but those freaks of nature seemed to find their own feed higher up the mountain range. The more she tracked them, the more impossible the task became, not just because of the rocky terrain but also because each seemed to be larger and more fierce than any cow she'd ever encountered. She'd thought she was purchasing a Charolais-Hereford cross, a hardy, disease-resistant hybrid that could grow to a thousand pounds in a season. She was wrong.

In desperation, she'd had five separate outfits come to the ranch, spy a couple of the cattle, then turn away, saying that it wasn't worth the money to break their necks in such inhospitable terrain. In each case, the final edicts had been that if she really wanted to solve her problem, the cows needed to be destroyed, especially the bigger ones with horn spreads of nearly six feet. That wasn't an option to Clem.

Dead cows fetched no money at market, and if she could only *get* those suckers to market, they'd be rich.

"You should've chosen something a little tamer, smaller," the leader of the first outfit had remarked as he'd climbed back into his beat-up truck.

"Maybe they're Charolais, got the coloring," a man in the second had said. "But can't see no Hereford in them. Maybe longhorn."

"Gotta have some Brahman. Look at how mean they is," a third had offered with a shrug.

"Man, look at that horn spread. Think you could

have a strain of Belgian Blues." A member of the fourth had shaken his head in awe. "It's gold if you don't mind dying while mining it."

When the last outfit went, Clem was still left with enormous, renegade cows trampling the land, hiding in the crevasses, growing healthier, heavier and more territorial with each passing day, as disease resistant as the man who'd sold them to her had assured her. Clem had kicked herself a thousand times for not asking about temperament. She'd only seen the potential dollar signs. A swelling sense of pride that maybe this was something that she could do hadn't helped. Maybe her mother's faith wasn't misplaced—no matter what her father thought, no matter what *she* thought.

It seemed she'd waited a long time to hear her father praise her for something that she'd *done*. For years, she just had to walk into the room and her father would light up. Somewhere along the way as Daddy's little girl, she'd learned that she didn't have to *do,* anything, simply *being* was enough. It was a hard lesson to unlearn since she'd gone from the adoration of her father to the adoration of her husband. Claire Wells had tried to warn Clem, tried to get her to realize that she had to rely on herself, but Clem hadn't listened. She'd gone ahead and married Nick rather than finish college.

Clem understood intellectually what her mother was saying, but she'd liked the fact that Nick loved her the way her father did. It felt right to Clem. Nick had done an exceptional job of taking her father's place until he decided to leave her for his colleague. *Devastation* couldn't begin to describe her feelings. Suddenly, at thirty-two, she faced difficulties that most people dealt with at eighteen. How to live alone, how to *be* alone.

But with her mother's help, she realized that there were things she could do. She knew horses. While Nick had been having his affair, she'd been at the stable with Archie, a beautiful chestnut that Nick had given her for their sixth anniversary. She also knew how to rope and brand. But apparently, not how to choose a herd.

"So tell me who'd help me," she had finally asked. "There's got to be someone."

The cowboys she'd found had exchanged glances. One shrugged and another kicked at the dust.

"There *is* someone," Clem had said with hope.

"Yep."

"But, ma'am, you just might want to shoot these, take your losses and get a real job."

Clem could have laughed at the irony of it all. This was the only real job she was qualified for.

"I *have* a real job." Clem had glared at them. "Tell me who can help me."

A long silence followed while the cowboys eyed each other.

One finally asked the other, "Where'd we last see him?"

"El Paso."

"He was scouting those crazy horses of his."

"Ben Thorton still with him?"

"Nope. Heard they split up after...you know. Those Miller brothers, too."

"Who?" Clem asked again. "Give me a name."

"Can't vouch for him."

"Craziest son of a— Oops, sorry, ma'am."

"Didn't they single-handedly clear out the old Russell Saloon?"

"Did some jail time."

The oldest man shook his head. "I'd feel bad if something happened to you, ma'am. Even if you could find him, he won't help."

"Why not?" Clem had asked, her voice curt.

"Retired."

"Give me his name," Clem had begged. If he was alive, he could help her. She wasn't going to let an itty-bitty complication like retirement get in her way.

With a sigh, he said, "Scott. Dexter Scott. Trust me, ma'am, you'd be better off if you didn't find him."

Dexter Scott.

Clem had burned that name into her mind. She'd scoured old copies of *Western Horseman,* looking for something, *anything* about him, a mention in an article, a small ad. Ben Thorton and the Miller brothers, too. Tracking one of them could lead her to him. She went on the Internet to the different ranching Web sites. Posted on message boards, sought information during chats.

Finally, some kind soul sent her a brochure, an

old tattered brochure. Clem had treated it like a map to buried treasure, carefully taping the folds intact. And when she discovered the phone number was out of service, she'd used a magnifying glass to read the faded address. The next evening, last night, in fact, she'd driven off in search of Dexter Scott, the legend.

He didn't look much like a legend, not with that frown. Clem cleared her throat. "Um, have you ever considered coming out of retirement?"

"Nope." The answer was matter-of-fact, given with a disinterested glance in her direction.

That answer was unacceptable.

Clem stared at the man who was stroking the nose of the horse. Whether he knew it or not, her fate was in his hands. And she wasn't going to lose six hundred cattle worth at least a thousand dollars apiece. She could, however, give up forty percent of what they would bring in. It was an enormous amount of money. With her cut, she could pay off her debts and still make enough to buy the most sedate herd of Herefords she could find.

"I'm sorry, I can't take no for an answer." Her voice came out a little weaker than she'd planned. Where was the authority that her father talked with? She sounded like she was asking for permission.

The cowboy's lips twisted into what she thought was a smile, but since the brim of his hat shaded his face, she couldn't quite tell. "You'll have to."

He gave the horse a final pat on the nose, before saying, "Skooch." The horse lurched underneath her as, in almost one motion, he pulled himself up behind her and then lifted her up and deposited her snugly between his lap and the horn of the well-used saddle. A warm forearm wrapped around her rib cage. As he took the reins from her hand. With just a touch of his heels, he turned the horse and urged it into a trot back in the direction of the ranch.

Clem was too astonished to protest.

Not that she could protest even if she wanted to. Her body was already cinched to his lean frame, his chest pressed flat against her spine, and while he had pulled back in the saddle to give her as much room as he could, it was a tight squeeze.

She held her breath as the horse danced underneath them, not at all certain he liked this newest burden. She felt the man behind her squeeze the ribs of the horse to establish control.

"Relax, you'll be more comfortable." His voice was polite. "Break fewer bones if we get tossed."

"Okay." But her breath just didn't want to let go.

They rode in silence for a cautious few minutes. Clem knew he was testing the horse, seeing if it was willing to take them home. When the horse didn't protest, she felt the cowboy settle down behind her.

"So explain again how you got in?" His voice rumbled from deep within his chest, and Clem could feel it reverberate against her back.

"I just went through the gates," she said, trying not to sound as defensive as she felt.

''They're locked.''

''They're latched,'' she corrected him. ''Only the last one was locked.''

''And?''

''I climbed over. Left my truck there.''

''How'd you find the horse?''

''He found me on top of the gate.''

That seemed to be enough of an explanation because he was silent.

After another hundred yards, he demanded, ''So what is it you want from me?''

''I want you to be as good as your brochure says you are.''

She didn't know what she expected in response to her outburst, but a deep chuckle wasn't it.

''Nobody's as good as brochures says they are. They're brochures.''

Clem's stomach knotted up. ''I need you to be.''

''I'm retired.''

There was something in his voice, some sort of odd quality that made her not want to believe him. His forearm tightened around her ribs and Clem swallowed her protest. He may think he was retired, but there was some ember in his hazel eyes not yet snuffed out. Clem didn't know how to fan it, but she knew that she needed to. As she thought, she became very conscious of the rhythm of his body and the horse as they moved across the desert. Riding with him was hypnotic, reminiscent of when she'd ridden with her father.

On cold fall evenings, Jim Wells would zip them

both up in his large sheepskin jacket, keeping her warm as they rode to the high ridge of their property to watch the sun set before dinner. She could feel the cold on her nose and ears, the comfort of her father's heartbeat. Even when she got her own horse, they still rode to watch the sunset, but it wasn't the same.

She could almost purr with the memory. She didn't want to like the way this stranger's arm felt around her waist, acknowledge how secure she felt with him. She'd done that once before. She frowned in displeasure at her own reaction. Apparently, even after the divorce, she hadn't learned anything at all. She was still waiting for someone to keep her close.

CHAPTER TWO

CLEM JERKED AWAKE as they rode up to Dexter Scott's ranch, then stiffened when she realized she'd relaxed against him. He obliged her new posture by loosening his arm, though she could still feel his hand on the top of her hip. A dingy, two-story Victorian came into sight, along with dead patches of grass and flower beds long overgrown with wild roses and native plants. Dexter Scott apparently cared more for the comfort of his horses than himself, because three well-placed, well-kept stables and a barn made the old Victorian look more faded.

Clem couldn't help studying the layout of his training area. She smiled when she saw a corral of horses only a mother or Dexter Scott could love. How different than what she'd anticipated. She'd imagined a ranch rather like an elite racing stable with glossy-coated handsome horses prancing across acres of green lawn.

Glossy coats, yes. Handsome, no. Dexter Scott's horses sported eyes set too close or ears too big or markings just plain wrong. Rather than giving these horses an endearing quality, the physical imperfections made them look as if they were genetic throwbacks of the worst possible mix. Clementine refused to be disappointed. Now that she'd found him, she was going to make sure Dexter Scott was the legend she needed him to be.

"Guess I must've dozed off. I was driving all night," she apologized, mentally climbing a thicker branch of hope. First impressions were rarely the measure one should use to judge the character of a person or a situation, right? And she shouldn't judge the horses, either.

A large hand slid under her thigh.

"Off you go," Dexter said as he boosted her leg over the saddle horn. With his arm still around her waist, Clem was gently set down on the ground. From this perspective, Dexter Scott was enormous. He swung himself out of the saddle and led the horse to one of the stables. The horses in the corral tossed their heads in greeting. Clem stood for a moment, looking around, trying to get her bearings. Then, even though he didn't invite her, she followed him.

Dexter Scott was sliding the door with one hand, and just as she'd suspected, it opened with a quiet swish perfectly balanced on its rails like a finely made dresser drawer. She followed him as he led the horse to an empty stall. Yes, a man who kept his stables so clean could be an elite cowboy.

"So," Clem began. She climbed up on the lowest slat of the stall in order to see him better. "I need your help."

"Grab that hard brush for me, will you?" he asked her as he untied the leather knots of the saddle. He tended to his horse with practiced, methodical movements. With an easy heft, he put the saddle on a stall rail before he folded the horse blanket. Then with complete absorption, he ran his hand up and down the horse's back, up and down his legs, feeling for small stickers or other irritants.

A moment later Clem got the brush and handed it to him. With even circles, he began to curry the horse, getting rid of the dirt, gravel and bits of desert sand that had worked their way up under the saddle. After a protracted silence, Clem wondered if he'd actually heard her.

"I need your help," Clem repeated, mesmerized by his movements. His right hand brushed, while his left hand followed behind, lightly. Every so often, he paused to dig through the coarse hair to investigate before continuing. The horse stretched with the care and Clem could see the muscles ripple on its withers. With each stroke, Clem felt even more certain that this was the man she wanted, the man she needed.

After he finished one side, he moved to the other and as if synchronized, Clem picked up a softer finishing brush and went to work. The horse whinnied softly. Dexter Scott just kept brushing and feeling, feeling and brushing. Clem wondered if he paid attention to his wife the same way he paid attention to the horse.

"It's taken me a month to find you," Clem remarked, trying another way into the conversation. "I've driven all night from Los Banos."

His hat obscured everything but his mouth. "I know Los Banos."

Clem took that as an opening. "My dad has a ranch southwest of the city, right up against the Diablo range."

After another extended silence, Clem tried again. Maybe he was waiting for her to finish her thought.

"We have a few cows roaming up there I need to get down."

"A few?"

If she could see his face, she'd probably watch one of those dark eyebrows arch up.

"Well, six hundred."

He didn't say anything.

Finally, he pushed back the brim of his hat and asked, "What kind?"

His eyes were moss-green now. Clem looked away and brushed her side more vigorously, trying to cover the flush that was working its way up her neck. She muttered, "Don't really know."

For the first time, he stopped what he was doing and evaluated her. "How can you not know?" Curiosity tinged his voice.

DEXTER SCOTT HAD TO ADMIT he was interested. By the way she rode and brushed, she knew her way around horses. She also knew her way around gates. Some of his gates were constructed more than a hundred years ago, though the one closest to the property was new. That one he locked.

He took advantage of the fact that she wouldn't look at him. On closer examination, she didn't resemble Joanna so much. Her hands, for instance. Joanna's hands were like a basketball player's and since she'd never wore gloves, they were as weathered as old leather. But this woman's hands were smooth, soft, just showing signs of wear. Joanna would also have been able to tell the breed of a cow a hundred yards away. Who was she? Dexter realized he didn't even know her name.

"Who *are* you, anyway?" he demanded, appalled that his voice sounded as if it erupted from his belly.

She stopped currying as the flush spread from her slender neck to her ears. "I'm sorry. I should have introduced myself earlier. Clem. Clementine Wells.''

Clementine.

''The song or the orange?''

She made a face, then shrugged slim shoulders and smiled a smile that revealed white, even teeth. ''I think the song, but I know my mother is partial to tangerines.''

Dexter couldn't think of anything to say, but he was grateful that her name wasn't Joan or Jo or Jess.

Clementine. Clem.

They continued to brush.

''I'd be indebted if you'd just come to the ranch to look at my problem. See if there's anything you could do. There's a fortune waiting for anyone who can do this.''

Dexter didn't need a fortune. He had more than enough money to exist.

''I'd offer you, er, forty percent of what you bring in.''

Dexter, against his will, wanted to laugh. She wasn't a tough negotiator. In fact, she looked so hopeful Dexter thought that if he was a different kind of man, he'd take the forty percent and then some. But as it was, forty percent, fifty percent, a hundred percent meant nothing. He didn't need the money. Rather than prolong her misery, he said, his voice as abrupt and definite as he could make it, "I told you, I'm retired."

She blinked and Dexter noticed her eyes were the same color as the blue horse blanket he'd just removed. He didn't want to see the hope there dull, but it was necessary. He didn't work anymore and that was all there was to it.

There was another silence.

Finally, she said, still hopeful, "I have more than six hundred cattle out there, all weighing more than a thousand pounds. You'd have enough money to fix up your house."

Dex flinched at her insinuation that he was struggling financially. He had plenty of money to fix up the house. The cans of paint that Joanna had bought for the exterior were still in the basement, dusty, untouched. He was glad the pick in his hand didn't falter as he used quick, short movements to clean New Horse's back right hoof.

"It's a beautiful house."

He ignored her, wondering why this woman didn't seem put off.

"It's a shame that it should be so run-down. I imagine it was quite a showpiece in its day."

She stopped talking, but the barn wasn't silent to Dexter. He could hear the blood rushing through his head, New Horse's breathing, the woman's movements as she put away the brushes. He worked his way through the other three hooves, concentrating on a grooming ritual that he'd completed a thousand times.

CLEM WATCHED THE MAN straighten from his chore.

"No." The single word bit into the stillness.

"What?" Clem asked, pretending to play dumb. Maybe it had been wrong to make a remark about his house, but it was the truth. And she just couldn't accept "no" for an answer.

"No," he enunciated, and straightened. "Thanks, but no thanks. I'm retired. You have a safe drive back, ma'am."

She watched him look around as if he'd suddenly realized he'd finished the grooming, then stride out of the stall, having to wait impatiently for Clem to exit before he could shut the door. He walked out of the barn, heading for the house.

Clem stood there, her mind whirling as she sought a solution. It wasn't going to end this way. It wasn't. There must be something that he wanted that she could give him. She hadn't driven all night to be flicked away like a fly on the potato salad. His long stride had already taken him to the Victorian, where he climbed up the creaking steps, his arm extended to open the screen door.

"Hey!" she called in desperation. "Can I at least use your bathroom? It's a heck of a drive back."

She didn't think he heard her, but he stopped with his hand on the screen. He moved it back and forth, back and forth. Finally, without turning, he gave a quick nod and then disappeared into the house, the door banging behind him.

Clem smiled. If she got in the house, she would at least have another shot at convincing him.

When she stepped into the house, two things struck her; the darkness and the aroma of frying sausage and pancakes. Her stomach rumbled. She was starving. She'd driven all night and the only thing she'd eaten that morning was a quick sandwich and a cup of coffee at a fast-food restaurant in Barstow. What she wouldn't give for some of those pancakes and sausages.

"Hello?" she inquired, peering into the shadows, waiting for her eyes to adjust to the dimness.

No answer.

She supposed Dexter Scott figured she'd find her own way to the bathroom and then her own way out. She walked down the hall, looking at pictures that were covered in more than a layer of dust. Cobwebs strung the frames together, and Clementine frowned. What a sad, gloomy house. If she didn't know that he lived here, she would have thought it was abandoned. Any happiness that it had once known had long since leached out, leaving just a shell of a house. Maybe that was what was wrong with Dexter Scott—the fun, the adventure had leached out of him.

Clementine took a deep breath. All the more reason he should help her. It'd probably do him good not to have to live in this house, day in, day out.

She heard the clattering of dishes and the pleasant rumble of male voices. Surely that couldn't be Dexter Scott.

With a deep breath, she walked in to find him and two other cowboys seated at the rickety dining table, elbows up as they talked, washing their food down with dark coffee.

"Hi," she said.

Her words had the effect of a pause button on the VCR. All activity stopped; forks poised in the air, a cup of coffee stopped at a mouth. She felt as if they were watching her every move, but she didn't let that deter her.

"Hey, there." She greeted them. "That looks really good."

The motion started up, as the two cowboys—obviously related—exchanged glances. Forks came down, coffee was sipped, then white teeth gleamed.

"Ma'am," the one closest to her said with a nod.

"Hi, I'm Clementine Wells." She stuck out her hand to the one who had addressed her.

"Randy. Randy Miller." A big hand, slightly sticky, engulfed hers, but the grip was very gentle.

"Miller?" Clem felt some hope flare. They were part of the Dexter Scott package. They were the rough ones who'd done jail time that she should steer clear of. "Of the Russell Saloon fame?"

The brothers exchanged glances. Randy grinned and poked a thumb in the other cowboy's direction. "That was Ryan's fault."

"I was defending your honor." Ryan stood up and extended his hand. "Ryan Miller. Glad to meet you."

Less sticky but just as gentle. Clem felt a whole lot lighter. She ventured a quick glance in Dexter's direction. He was stirring milk into a cup of coffee, hard enough to create a racket with his spoon.

"The bathroom's down the hall. Second door to your right." He stopped stirring.

Randy grinned and Clem realized she did have to use the facilities. "Thank you. I'll be right back."

"Then you'll be on your way," Dexter said, his voice rough.

"Mmm-hmm." Clem hedged her bets. Maybe she could get a breakfast out of this. And another opportunity to convince him.

"SO WHERE DID SHE COME FROM?" Randy asked as he leaned over the table.

Dexter stuffed a forkful of pancakes in his mouth even though they tasted like straw. He swigged some of the coffee and then added more syrup to the stack and took another bite.

One trait that this woman, Clementine, and Joanna had in common was the fact they couldn't take "no" for an answer. Even when he'd said "no" to Joanna, she'd thought it meant "maybe," and then through sheer persistence made him change the "maybe" to an "I'll think about it," eventually ending up with an "okay, with stipulations," which Joanna had ignored, anyway.

He didn't want to smile, but he couldn't help it. Joanna had been the only person who really knew him, who could see past his dark moods, who could make him laugh at the most dire of times. Seven years older, he'd taken care of her forever, shielding her from their father's abuse, telling her stories about their long-gone mother. Those stories were lies. Their mother had left them when Joanna was just a baby. Their father had never been the same. And when he'd taken an unnatural interest in Joanna's ten-year-old body, Dexter had left with Joanna in tow. They'd ridden three buses to get to Las Vegas, where Uncle Grubb, their father's older brother, had met them at the bus station and brought them here. For the first time ever, Dexter and Joanna had known what it was to live in a real home, the same Victorian their father had grown up in. Dex had slept in the attic Grubb had remodeled, because he believed a teenage boy needed his privacy, while Joanna had lived in a fairy-tale alcove.

Since Grubb didn't have children, he showered a lifetime of love on his newly acquired niece and nephew. When he died, he'd made Joanna and Dexter equal partners in the ranch. At the time, Dex and Ben Thorton were getting their business together. Joanna met Randy and Ryan and talked them into joining. Convincing Randy had been easy. Soon he and Joanna were inseparable.

After Joanna's death, the ranch had become as desolate and bleak as Dex felt. He certainly didn't need some woman with a stubborn chin and big blue eyes lighting up a room that he'd dimmed on purpose. He'd hoped she'd gotten the message and would be gone as soon as possible.

No such luck.

Before he could think to protest, Randy had invited her for some pancakes, which she accepted, seating herself right next to him.

He stared at the nicks in the table.

"I'm starving," she confessed, with a shy glance toward him, which he tried to ignore as well. That didn't seem to daunt her at all. She just held out a plate toward Ryan, who heaped it full with sausage, scrambled eggs and pancakes.

"Enough!" Clem protested with a giggle. "I'll waddle my way home."

It almost hurt to hear feminine laughter.

"You're leaving after you eat those," Dexter told her.

She stared at him with those large eyes fringed with dark lashes, and then nodded, her eyes cast down in acquiescence.

Dexter didn't believe it for a second. To make sure that she left after she ate, he would escort her out to her vehicle himself and watch until he couldn't see her taillights any more.

"And where is home?" Randy asked her.

"Los Banos."

"Pretty country," Ryan commented.

Clem nodded. "I've just moved back to my father's ranch. He and my mother retired to Arizona last summer."

"And what brings you way out here?"

There was a long pause, and Dexter found that he'd stopped eating, because even though he knew what she had to say, he liked the way she spoke, as if she had to force herself to speak louder to be heard.

"I bought some cattle that've gone feral on me in a year."

"Really, now?" Ryan perked up. "How many?"

"Lots. Over six hundred."

"And?" Randy asked, his voice speculative.

"I've come to ask Mr. Scott if he'd like the job."

"Dex's retired."

Dexter bristled. Funny, how he'd spent the morning trying to convince her that she was barking up the wrong tree, and now that Randy had confirmed it— Well, hell. He didn't need Randy talking for him.

"You are retired, aren't you, Dex?" Ryan asked, a speculative look in his eyes.

Dexter didn't say anything. He knew what his friends were doing. They'd been trying to get him back into the business, telling him life went on even after death. Randy had said as much, but Dexter didn't want to believe it. It still hurt too much—not just Joanna's death or the massive hole that her presence left, but the undeniable knowledge that he'd caused it.

"Even ballplayers come out of retirement," Clementine said. Then she took one look at his expression and turned her attention to Randy. "Since Mr. Scott isn't available, maybe you and your brother would think about taking the project on. I've heard just as many good things about you. I'm offering forty percent."

"How big did you estimate those cows were?" Randy asked.

"Conservatively— A thousand pounds. I think there are several up to fifteen hundred pounds."

"In a season?" Ryan was skeptical. "I don't think so."

Clem shrugged. "I didn't think so, either, but unless there were six hundred cows with our brand that we forgot to pick up last year, these are the ones I put out in October."

"When would you need us to start?" Randy asked.

Dexter had been doing fine with the conversation. He'd been eating breakfast, minding his own business, disregarding the pointed looks his friends gave him, ignoring the fact that if he didn't look down he'd be staring at the soft curve of Clementine Wells's neck. But he coughed with Randy's question. No. Randy couldn't be thinking about taking the job.

"I thought you guys had sworn to take a couple weeks off before starting up again," Dexter finally said.

All eyes turned to him.

Clem ignored his outburst. "I'd really like to get the cows in before Thanksgiving. I know that doesn't give you much resting time, but my parents are coming back for the holiday, and it'd be nice to have this problem taken care of."

Ryan grinned. "Thanksgiving? It's only September."

"You don't know these cows," Clem said, her voice ominous.

"You have any men to help us?"

Dexter made a noise of protest, but no one acknowledged that, either.

Clem nodded. "Three, I know I could call on if we had real work. I could ask around."

Randy looked at Ryan for confirmation. "No. I think the five of us can do some considerable damage. Ryan?"

Ryan shrugged. "Why not?"

"Okay, Ms. Wells."

"Clem, call me Clem, please." She gave them a relieved smile and attacked her stack of pancakes. "Thank you. You don't know what your help means to me. Thank you."

Dexter couldn't stand her effusive gratefulness anymore. He got up and went outside without a word.

THE ORANGE JUICE IN THEIR cups vibrated from Dexter's abrupt departure, and a silence fell over the table. Clem ate as rapidly as she could, trying not to mind that he'd left so quickly.

"You should slow down," Ryan cautioned her. "You'll get indigestion."

Clem looked up into his sympathetic eyes. "I've overstayed my welcome."

"It's not that," Randy told her. "You just caught him by surprise. You caught all of us by surprise." He studied her face. "Though I'm wondering if this isn't the best thing for him."

Clem wiped her mouth and then stood up to take her dish to the sink.

Ryan intercepted her, taking the plate from her. "Don't worry about that, we've got it."

"Thank you so much for the breakfast and for considering the job. It seems as if I've searched a long time for men like you." Clem scribbled her name and phone number on a scrap of paper by the sink. "You'll call me when you're ready to come?"

The brothers nodded. "Probably by the end of the week."

"Where's your car?" Randy asked.

"Truck," Clem said. "Out by the last gate. I walked in. Well, rode in, when I found the brown horse."

Randy looked at her hard. "What brown horse?"

"The nice one with the white star," Clem smiled. "He's a sweetie."

Both brothers snorted.

"What?" she asked.

They exchanged glances with each other. Then Randy laughed with a rueful shake of his head. "I bet that stuck in his craw. New Horse doesn't usually like to be ridden. Ms. Wells—"

"Clem, please." Clementine insisted.

"Clem, I'll drive you back," Randy said, fishing the keys out of his pocket.

"Thank you. You *will* call, right?" She looked for affirmation from one or the other, but both nodded at the same time, wide smiles transforming their faces.

"Expect us at the end of the week."

When Randy pushed open the screen door for her, Clem saw Dexter leaning up against a porch rail, staring pensively at the corral of horses. He didn't look up.

"I'll just be running Clem back to her truck," Randy said, keys rattling.

Clem didn't even think Dexter heard until he pulled himself off the rail. He put an arm out to block Randy's way.

"I'll take her" was all he said.

Clem looked over her shoulder at Randy, who just smiled and shrugged. Without waiting for her, Dexter Scott had already taken the three steps off the porch and was striding toward his truck.

"You coming?" he asked as he paused at the passenger side, yanking open the door.

Clem forced herself to walk, not trot, to where Dexter was putting a shotgun on the rack behind the seat. The shortness of his movements screamed his impatience.

"Thank you," Clem said as he boosted her up. Lord, he was strong. She could feel his fingers, as if they were each individually imprinted on her upper arm. "I could have ridden with Mr. Miller." Clem pushed the assortment of papers on the seat across to the middle before she sat down.

"I want to make sure you're going to leave," he said as he climbed in next to her. He indicated the wad of oil-stained rags Clem held in her hands. "Just put those on the floor."

Clem dropped them at her feet.

"I *am* leaving." She hunted for the seat belt. It was the dustiest truck that she'd ever been in, clearly not equipped for passengers. She was sure there would be bottom imprints where she sat. Disposable soda cups were everywhere, giving Clem a good idea what fast food he favored when he was on the road. She lifted off the seat and pried out a pencil from the seam between the seat and the backrest, before positioning herself as far away as she could get from him, keeping her posture very straight. His quick glance told her that he noticed.

"I *did* find your horse for you." Clem couldn't keep the asperity out of her voice as he turned the key.

The engine revved.

"And I did provide you a way home, so you didn't have to walk," Clem reminded him.

When he spun the truck into a tight turn, she held on to the pipe that he'd rigged as a door handle.

"And I know first aid, so if you were hurt, I was prepared to patch you up."

With that said she lapsed into prim silence.

It didn't matter one bit that he wasn't going to respond, though she did notice that contrary to the fast spin, they were moving at an awfully slow pace toward her truck. She glanced at his speedometer. Their speed didn't even register.

"The faster you go, the faster I'll be out of here," she said, and braved a full look at him.

Her heart stopped.

He was smiling, or at least she thought he was smiling. There were crinkles in the corners of his eyes and his lips were definitely tilted up.

"And in return, I didn't shoot you," Dexter replied.

"Well, that's true," Clem agreed. "But that was because I had your shotgun."

"I was close enough to get it back, if I wanted it. I could have shot you out in the desert and left you for dead."

"You wouldn't do that." Clem was positive. Even though he'd been none too friendly, his smile did odd, fluttery things to her chest.

He gave her a sidelong look. "And what makes

you so sure? You know, a female all alone isn't necessarily safe."

She'd had that thought herself. But she'd forced herself to keep going. She'd *found* him, even though he didn't want to be found. "Sometimes it's not always a good thing to be safe."

"Safety is a human need," he said.

Clem nodded and saw that her truck was indeed closer, even though it seemed as if he'd actually stopped. "True. But I've been safe all my life. This was one time that I thought more about what I needed to do than what would be safe. And I got what I wanted. Your friends are coming to help me."

There was a long pause. Clem could hear the tires crunch over the gravel.

Finally, Dexter admitted, "They're good men. The best. If you have a cow problem, they'll be able to fix it."

Maybe it was a note in his voice, maybe it was the way that he furrowed his brow, but something made Clem want to reach out and pat his arm. Instead, she blurted, "You sure you don't want to come, too?"

For a moment, no longer than it took to blink, Clem swore that he did. He studied her and Clem felt the familiar flush creep up her neck.

"You blush easy."

Clem didn't know how to answer that. "It's because I'm so fair."

"Or you're shy."

"Maybe. That's safe, too, huh?"

"Shyness?"

She nodded. "Sure. If I'm shy, I don't have to risk meeting new people. Shy is like those gates that you've got. They minimize the chance of people intruding. Seems as if we're alike that way."

Dexter didn't say anything, and after a moment they were at the gates.

Clem struggled to open the door.

"The old handle broke," he explained. "Let me." He leaned over, his arm brushing up against her legs. With an easy jerk, he popped the door open. While he was at it, he unclipped her seat belt.

"Thanks."

"No problem."

She saw him getting out and assured him, "I'll be fine. I promise I won't bother you anymore."

"How are you going to get through the gate?" he asked, his voice dry.

"The same way I got in. I'll climb over it." She gave him a big grin.

He held up a key. "Save your energy. You've got a long drive back."

She waited as he crouched down next to the lock. It was hard to believe that she was never going to see him again. She resisted the urge to lay her hand on his shoulder, to run the back of her hand along the soft skin under his collar.

He released the padlock and stood up, swinging open the gate. "There you go, ma'am."

"I guess I should thank you for not shooting me." She made her tone as light as possible, as she stepped past him, but it was hard because her lips felt dry and dusty. She licked them, not at all sure why she was possessed with the overwhelming urge to kiss this man. Was it the loneliness in his eyes? Her heart thumped harder at the thought. She knew about being lonely even when surrounded by other people, about being lonely even when you were married or sleeping in the same bed with someone. Maybe Dexter Scott had chosen solitude. Maybe he'd chosen to erect the fences around his property, but no one, not even Dexter Scott, would choose loneliness.

His eyes were trained on her face, as if he could read her thoughts. She focused on his lips.

It'd been so very long since she'd had a real kiss. There'd be nothing to regret, because kissing Dexter Scott would be merely a crowning regret on the top of the six hundred regrets running around on her father's property.

Besides, she'd never see him again.

CHAPTER THREE

AS CLEARLY AS IF SHE HAD already kissed him, she could feel his stubble under her hand. Heat reflected off his clear eyes and she stepped toward him. As if choreographed, Dexter met her, and she wrapped her arms around his neck, feeling the solid muscles. He flinched just slightly and she remembered his tender shoulder.

"Sorry," she murmured.

"What for?" His voice was right in her ear, low, husky. She could feel the moist warmth of his mouth right at the curve of her jawline.

"Your shoulder."

"It's fine." He held her tighter as if to prove to her there was nothing wrong with his shoulder. The weight of his arm against her waist was reassuring. His hand was splayed across the small of her back, warming her. It had been a long time. Perhaps a lifetime. She didn't remember having this feeling with Nick, not ever. Not even on their wedding night.

Dex's face was so close she could see the individual pores that the rough stubble grew out of. She inhaled, smelling saddle wax, sweat, dust. It was a dangerous combination. Clem became fascinated by the slight cleft in his chin, the indentations in his profile, the distinct cupid's bow, the dimple that flickered in and out. He seemed to have stopped breathing and was waiting.

Simply waiting.

"This isn't what shy women do," he informed her with a low, guttural whisper. "Kiss strange men."

His words should have jerked her back to reality, but right now, she couldn't think, all she could do was feel the strength of his arm behind her, the heat of his body in front of her, the brush of his powerful thighs, supporting the both of them, because she was certain that if he let go, she'd fall over.

"I haven't kissed you yet." She searched his eyes, which he tried to shutter.

DEXTER FROZE. Instead of letting go, as he intended, he found himself pulling this woman, this Clementine, closer to him, just to feel her press up against him.

Let go, his rational mind hollered at him. *Just let go and step back. Okay,* it finally conceded, *if you can't step back, just let go. You can step back in a second.*

Too late.

He felt her lips graze his, the heat of even that slight contact exploding in his chest. Bad idea. This was what playing with fire meant. He felt like a moth, fluttering up against a stark lightbulb, drawn to the very thing that would cause the destruction of all his walls. He didn't move, but rather lowered his head. If exploring that tender bottom lip of hers was going to be his destruction, then so be it.

His mouth covered hers, tentatively at first and then with the intensity of a moth that had been too long without light. She moaned and pulled herself onto her toes, her fingers stroking his neck and shoulders in a concentric circle that was making it hard to think. His eyes began to flutter closed, and then she was gone.

CLEM JERKED BACK, gulping for air, trying to pretend the kiss wasn't the best kiss she'd ever had and wondering what else she'd been missing. If someone had told her Dexter Scott would one day kiss her the way he just had, she would have never married Nick. She would have waited for Dexter Scott, even if it took him years to find her. Incredible. What an incredible kiss. Clementine felt her cheeks burn.

"Sorry about that. I don't know what got into me," she apologized. She hunted around in her jacket pocket for her keys, too embarrassed to even look at him.

"Don't be." The words were gruff.

She looked up and saw that his pupils were dilated. He took the keys from her hand and walked the two steps to her truck and opened up the door.

Wordlessly, Clem climbed in, unable to sort out the feelings churning inside her chest. She didn't want to leave him. She wanted to see him again. Then she laughed. Los Banos and Barstow were far apart. A long-distance relationship would never work. She rolled down the window and then started up the truck.

"I guess this is goodbye," she said.

"I guess so."

"You sure you don't want to come out and see my cows?"

There was a long pause.

Finally, he shut her door with a controlled slam and said, his voice short, "I'm retired."

WITH CURIOUS ANTICIPATION Clem stepped into a clean pair of just-for-company blue jeans. When she'd gotten home the other day, she'd slept for sixteen hours. It was the first good sleep she'd had in a long time. Randy Miller had called her the following afternoon to confirm their arrival time today. She would be so glad to see them, so glad that she would be able to hoist this particular burden onto their very capable shoulders. She didn't ask about Dexter Scott, or invite him again, but she couldn't help but think that it was his phone number Randy had given her. After this was over, she could always call him.

And then do what?

She was as inept at this as a sixth grader.

She shook off thoughts of Dexter Scott and his kiss as she fastened around her neck a gold heart locket that her father had given her on her sixteenth birthday. She needed to focus on her guests. Ryan had phoned earlier and told her to expect them at four o'clock. She'd spent most of the late morning and early afternoon cooking a supper she hoped would make her mother proud. A roast was slow simmering along with new potatoes, boiler onions and carrots. She'd made up a batch of coleslaw and prepared green beans, then she'd baked plenty of buttery garlic biscuits.

She hurried down the stairs, giving the dining room table another critical look. Her grandmother's china and silver looked nice on the lace tablecloth. It was a big table for three, but the floral centerpiece she'd had specially made in town compensated for the expanse.

Clem pulled open the kitchen door to check on the roast. Frijole, her elderly tabby, was lying in a particularly comforting sunbeam and meowed her disapproval. She got up, arched her back and gave a languid stretch, her front paws fully extended, her toes splayed. Then she straightened and looked expectantly at Clem.

"Sorry, girl," Clem said, and picked up the tabby. Clem felt her pulse slow considerably as she stroked Frijole. "Don't you know company's coming?" She buried her face into the soft fur. Frijole had absorbed many tears these past few years.

With the roast simmering and nothing left to do, Clem sat in her parents' living room and stared at the floor-to-ceiling stone fireplace. Should she start a fire? She nixed the idea. It wasn't cool enough yet. A moment later, she found herself hopping up to the door to see if she could detect any activity on the dirt road. At four-thirty, she moved to the porch, where she'd have a much better view of oncoming vehicles. Frijole joined her, plopping her twenty pounds on Clem's lap. When the sun started to fade, she fingered the cell phone number Randy had given her.

Clem got up and paced the length of the porch. She'd faxed them a detailed map, and they'd assured her they were familiar with the area. The phone rang inside the house, startling her as it echoed off the high ceilings. Cowchip, her parents' toothless fifteen-year-old Australian shepherd, began to bark. Clem shot through the door and lunged for the phone.

"Hello?" Clem asked breathlessly.

"Gate's locked."

Clem felt her heart clog her throat as adrenaline rushed through her veins. The voice sent a dozen light fingers down the fine hairs on her nape. She couldn't help the smile that spread across her face.

"W-what?" Maybe she was wrong. Maybe it was just Randy or Ryan.

"Gate's locked," the voice repeated. "Can't get through."

She wasn't mistaken. That voice was branded into her mind along with his kiss.

"Mr. Scott."

"Ms. Wells."

"I thought you were retired."

"Gate's still locked." He evaded her comment. He was here. He'd ventured outside the safety of his gates.

"Climb over," she joked.

The silence on the other side told her he didn't find that funny.

She added, "I'm coming right out. I thought I left it unlocked. Maybe one of the neighbors saw it and closed it up." She was rambling, but she couldn't help it. She was just so excited.

She hurried to her truck, pausing a moment to boost Cowchip into the back.

"Thank you, God," she whispered as she bounced down the road. She didn't know what she was thanking him for, the help or Dexter Scott. Nine miles and two gates later, she arrived at the fence just a mile off the main road and laughed with relief when she saw one pink and one dusty-brown truck, both with trailers hitched behind. The men were standing outside, talking and chuckling, their hats tilted low on their heads.

"Hi!" she said as she slid out of the cab of her truck. Cowchip hopped out with her to greet the strangers. She brushed her hair back, unintentionally making eye contact with Dexter. Her face hot, she bent down to find the lock. Clem felt her hands tremble as she fumbled to put the key in it.

Cowchip had managed to wriggle through the fence, and dogs started to bark in the back of one of the trailers. Horses whinnied. Cowchip snuffled Dexter Scott's jeans and boots, her tongue hanging out in happiness as Dex leaned over to scratch her behind her ears. Clem couldn't help watching. Even Cowchip fell victim to those hands, competent and calm, able to lull any unsuspecting being into a state of sedated rapture.

"You made it." She couldn't stop the breathy

quality in her voice, and she tried to cover it up by yanking off the lock and swinging open the gate.

Dexter straightened, uncurling to stand at his full height, his shoulders expanding like the wingspan of a hawk. The smile he had for Cowchip disappeared, replaced with a look much more speculative as his gaze flickered up and down, pausing at the heart locket. Her hand came up to touch it. He continued to stare, as if he were taking in every detail of her, his eyes finally settling on her mouth. He remembered the kiss, Clem realized. If possible, her face felt hotter. Clem turned to the Miller brothers.

"Are you a sight for sore eyes," Clem said, leaning over to shake their hands heartily.

Randy laughed. "I bet we are. I figured you wouldn't mind if we brought along extra baggage." He elbowed Dexter in the back, but he ignored Randy and got back into his truck and then gunned the engine.

Clem took that as her cue. She moved her truck on to the gravel road so they could pull around her. Then she shut and relocked the gate before jumping into the truck to catch up with them. At the next gate, she felt as if she was all fingers, knowing Dexter was watching her every movement. When she finally got the latch undone, she glanced up at him and he tipped his hat in acknowledgement, then drove past her.

By the time they'd gone through the last gate and arrived at the house, Clem was very relieved. They got out of their trucks, looking around.

"Beautiful area." Ryan whistled.

Clem nodded. "Thanks." She walked toward the main house. "Come in, please."

Randy shook his head. "We need to let the horses and the dogs out. They've been cooped up for long enough. They need a good stretch. It probably wouldn't be a bad idea to let the horses out in the corral for a while, just to get the kinks out of their legs."

"Of course," Clem agreed. "Do you need help?"

"No. We've got it." Randy was already starting to unlatch the trailer. Ryan was right behind him, letting the dogs out the side door.

The dogs barked with enthusiasm and raced up and down the courtyard, releasing hours of pent-up energy.

"Any preferences where we put the horses?" Ryan asked, leading out a beautiful mahogany horse, obviously not one of Dexter's.

Clem shook her head. "Either corral is fine." She pointed west. "I emptied that stable for all your horses. I hope there's enough room. If not, you're welcome to any free space."

Dexter looked up at the sky. "A few can stay

out. They might prefer it. Give them a chance to get used to the air."

A shrill, terrified screech grabbed their attention. The dogs were chasing Frijole, who moved quite swiftly considering her bulk, scrambling under the trailer ramp, only to startle New Horse, who was being led out by Randy.

"Quince! Bam-Bam! Dell! *Come!*" Dexter commanded, sharpness in his voice.

Then a sharp epithet shot out of Randy as he clutched his face. New Horse was free.

Clem ran toward New Horse, who was intent on trampling Frijole. The cat squalled in defense, teeth bared, her body hunched, prepared to both attack and retreat at the same time. Clem walked with careful purpose toward the brown horse, crooning to him, reassuring him that the cat wouldn't hurt him. But even though the horse's ears pricked up at the sound of her voice, his eyes were wild and his hooves were ready to flatten the cat.

As if in slow motion, Dexter saw New Horse rear again when Clem stepped in to rescue the cat. And he felt raw fear trickle down the back of his neck like sweat.

What the hell was she doing?

She was going to be crushed.

Fear became terror. He was suffocating as he stood there watching her sweep up the cat and duck under New Horse, the horse's hooves just inches from her head. She stumbled, barely clinging to the cat and her balance. But somehow, she kept her footing.

"It's not the horse's fault," Dexter heard in a fog as Clem reassured the cat. "He's just a little spooked. I'd suggest, Frijole, if you want to live out the few lives you have left, you keep clear of the dogs and the horses while they're here." With a quick kiss to the furry head, Clem let go of the cat, who sensibly took off for the safety of the bunkhouse. Then she walked up to the frenzied horse and caught his reins.

Dexter saw her arms strain against the power of the horse, but she kept crooning to him as she moved as close to him as she could.

Come on, Dex, help me bring in that cow.

Joanna's clear tones came to him as if she were standing right there.

"Joanna, slow down. You're going too fast. When we get the time, we'll get her. Come on back! We'll do it tomorrow."

"Tomorrow-shamorrow. That's what you said yesterday and the day before that. If you won't get the job done, I will. She's getting away, Dex. Come on, do I have to do everything myself?"

"I knew I shouldn't have let you sweet-talk me—"

"Oh, Dexter!" Her voice had been filled with fun and exasperation. *"Come on!"*

"Joanna! Stop!"

Dexter felt the words stick in his throat just as they'd done three years ago. He'd just sat on his horse, frozen as she'd disappeared over the edge of the ravine. Her terrified scream and the shriek of her horse still echoed in his head. He hadn't wanted to look, because he knew what he would find.

"Where is she?" Randy had reined his horse in next to Calisto, frantic in his search for Joanna.

Dexter just looked in the direction of the ravine, and Randy took off as if he was propelled by a slingshot.

"Is she okay?" Ryan was right behind his brother.

Dexter couldn't speak.

Randy's sobs were the only sounds he heard after that.

"Where do you want me to put him?"

"What?" Dexter was jerked out of the painful reverie. Clem was right next to him, her hand light on the reins of the now-calm horse.

"Are you okay? You're really pale." She peered up at him, her eyes inquiring.

"Don't do that again." Dexter bit out the words as he yanked the reins out of her hands. He strode away, leading the horse to the farthest corral.

CLEM STARED AT DEX. He hadn't touched her but she felt like she'd been slapped. Her chest hurt, or was that just her feelings? She wasn't certain what she wasn't supposed to do again. Try to save her cat? Well, too bad. She wasn't about to let Frijole meet her demise that way. She just wouldn't.

"What the hell were you thinking? Or were you even thinking?" Dexter had returned and the anger in his voice managed to push her most volatile button. "Risking your life for a stupid cat."

Ordinarily, Clem would have winced and felt as if she'd broken a basic rule, but this time she turned on him, her nose to his, well, chest.

"I'm not about to let my cat get trampled," Clem insisted, not really understanding where the power in her voice came from. She added, "Things are fine. And for the record, she's not a stupid cat. She's more reliable than my husband ever was."

She glanced up and then looked away, trying to control the anger that seemed to have erupted out of nowhere. She never argued. She hated to argue. She avoided arguments whenever and wherever possible. But this fury seemed to bubble up and over.

Dexter's eyes flickered over her face and Clem didn't know why but she got the impression he'd just finished an evaluation of his own. She didn't want to think about what he thought of her.

"Just stay out of that horse's way," he said, all his anger dissipated. His eyes searched hers for a long time, then he added, "Please."

WITH HER POT ROAST in one hand and the coleslaw in the other, Clem took a deep breath and entered the dining room to find that Randy, Ryan and Dexter had taken over her beautiful table. The china plates and silverware were pushed to the side, and the centerpiece was now on an end table, where it was perched right in front the fire. A variety of land maps were spread out over the table and the three men pored over them. She looked over their shoulders as she set down the roast. It didn't take her long to locate the main house and her father's property on the land maps.

Randy was stabbing at a mountain peak with a biscuit. Strawberry preserves leaked onto it. He looked none the worse for his encounter with New Horse's head, except for a nasty bruise that was traveling up his cheek toward his eye.

"Jeez, Rand, put it in your mouth," Ryan told him, while he used the edge of his lace napkin to clean off the map, smearing red across the bottom. "You don't know what I had to go through to get these."

"I still tell you, this time of the year they'll be as high up as they can get. That's where the feed is.'' Randy chewed and swallowed, then took the coleslaw out of Clem's hands and made a place for it on the table. Dexter began to pass the plates around. ''Especially with such an early rain. I've never seen these hills so green, so early.''

Randy was right, Clem realized as she went back for the green beans and an extra place setting. Usually it wasn't until the spring when the mountain range that separated the San Joaquin Valley from the San Benito Valley turned from the brown-paper-bag color burned into it by the scorching heat of the summer to a rich emerald green. She'd been out there getting burned, too, trying to get in the last of the cows. She hadn't even realized that the moderate temperatures had tricked the rolling hills into thinking that spring was just around the corner. It wouldn't last. The freeze of December would kill off anything green. But those cows would probably continue to grow, just to spite her.

She placed the green beans on the table and sat on the chair next to Ryan, kitty-corner from Dexter. She tried to make herself as obscure as possible, until Ryan passed her a plate of pot roast that Randy had carved with easy expertise.

Ryan continued to blot strawberry preserves off the map. Then he nodded. ''I don't think they'll risk getting caught in a gully when the rains come in.

They must be feeling the humidity in the air. Did anyone check the forecast?''

''I did,'' Clem volunteered, and flushed at Ryan's look of approval. She scooped up some green beans.

''And what's it say?'' Randy asked.

''Clear until the end of next week. There's a high-pressure system off the Pacific that's building steam. Big rains from then on.''

Randy and Ryan exchanged glances. ''That doesn't give us much time.''

''A window of about a week.'' Dex finally spoke, then refocused their attention on the mountain peak. ''How do you propose we even get there?'' He put a generous portion of coleslaw on his plate and took three more biscuits.

''A service road,'' Clem said, peering over Ryan's shoulder. Her voice came out loud and she tried not to feel self-conscious about inserting herself into their conversation as if she had a perfect right to be there. She leaned over, and pointed to an area on the map right in front of Dexter, tracing it with her index finger. She tapped another quadrant. ''I've spotted a bunch of them right here by Peckham's Ridge, but by the time we found a way to get to them, they were long gone. I think they moved up this way toward Wright's Peak.''

''How far does the road go?'' Ryan asked, studying the map with interest. Clem could see him thinking, and an overwhelming sense of respect flooded through her.

''Far enough,'' Clem said as she sat down again. She popped a carrot in her mouth, chewed, then swallowed before saying. ''Once you're out that far, you'll need to ride in, anyway. We tried to set up a corral there this summer, but then we couldn't figure out how to get the cows there. There's a narrow creek bed that's dry during the summer, but during the spring we couldn't even get past it. So the cows were stuck on the other side of the ridge. Then they went up.''

''No other way to get them in?'' That was Randy.

''If we used a helicopter, we could transport them across the reservoir, but before you say anything, don't think that I didn't calculate the cost.''

''Is the creek running yet?'' Dexter asked. He had worked his way through his first helping of pot roast and was sopping up the gravy with his biscuit.

''Just barely. The rain last month was enough to soak the land, but it's just a trickle.''

''Until next week.''

Randy and Dexter exchanged looks. ''We could get them to the valley and then lead them through.''

''One by one?'' Ryan shook his head. He cocked his head toward Clem. ''How many'd you estimate you have?''

Clem inhaled and wondered if she should lie. She

then met Dexter's clear eyes and swallowed. Once they were in the mountains they'd know, anyway. "Over six hundred. Probably more, since I think they have offspring now. I put out fifteen hundred last September. And we went in May to get them back."

"And could only get nine hundred?"

"Eight hundred forty-three. We found twenty-six dead, mostly falls."

Ryan pursed his lips in a silent whistle. "That's still a truckload. In a week."

"We've done it before," Randy reminded him. "Remember Ojai?"

"But that was in late summer. We didn't have to worry about rain."

"But it didn't take us much more than three or four days to get the entire herd in."

"Yeah, by luck more than anything else," Ryan said dryly.

"When did you know you were in trouble?" Randy asked Clem. She looked around and all eyes, even Dexter's, were trained on her, waiting for her to answer.

Clem cleared her throat. "When something that'd taken my father two weeks to do in the past was taking two months. Good thing I started in early March. I thought for sure that I'd have them down by May, even considering my relative inexperience.

I also saw that it was coming at a high cost. We exhausted our horses, the few dogs we had. We also lost a couple of dogs to cows that were more aggressive than we expected."

"Aggressive?"

She shrugged. "They attacked. They turned and charged us, as if they knew that if they worked together, there was nothing we could do but run."

"Which you did."

"You bet." She couldn't help but smile. "I'm obsessed, but I do want to live."

She didn't want to think any more about the past summer. She'd lost most of the dogs to heatstroke. After they got that first group of cows in, she had three of her father's cowboys quit on her. She pushed her beans around on her plate.

"Sorry, Clem, your daddy's been good to me, but I've got a family."

Clem couldn't blame them. She didn't want to face the cows, either, but even with their advanced size, the ones they'd brought in had just carried the ranch through the summer. She hadn't had anything left over to invest in new calves. The few times she'd gone into the mountains by herself, she'd realized that this job was way beyond her. She'd spent the latter part of the summer and the beginning of the fall searching for someone who could help her.

''We'd need to set up two corrals and lead them out, corral by corral.'' Ryan said.

''Maybe three.'' Dex nodded.

''Do we have enough?''

''We have enough fencing for two,'' Randy said. ''But we can dismantle the first and make it the third.''

''We have a portable one, also,'' Clem put in.

''Do you think we could herd them?'' Dexter asked Clem directly.

''If you could find them, *you* might be able to—as long as you've got steel-plated chaps for you and full body armor for your horse.''

No one spoke, and she realized that they really didn't believe her.

''You think I'm making this up?''

The men looked at one another and shifted uncomfortably.

''Not exactly.'' Ryan spoke first. ''We've just been around a lot more cows than you have, and we've seen some hostile ones, but haven't yet come across a breed that charges in herds.''

''A stampede, maybe,'' added Randy. ''But not direct charging, like to scatter anything.''

''These charged,'' Clem insisted. She stood up, her face red. Even her father hadn't believed her when she'd described what had happened. He'd just verbally patted her on the back and suggested she call some of his friends to help her.

"You thought they charged. Something might have spooked them from behind." Dex's voice was placating.

"We'll have to find out how they're organized," Randy remarked.

"*If* they are organized," Ryan said.

"All I know is that they've scattered all over the property and then some. And I just didn't have the muscle power or the dogs to enclose them. Now I'm not even certain about the ratio of bulls to cows."

Dex's face didn't quite mask his disgust. "Didn't you check your herd?"

Clem felt her cheeks get hot, but replied in an even voice. "I had help that wasn't nearly as careful as they should have been. And I was so blinded by the notion of the big profit rolling into my bank account that I didn't *care* what kind of cows I had. I just wanted to get them out to that great feed up there."

She tapped another spot on the map to show them where. "Even when we went up to check on them in January, and I saw how big they were getting, I didn't do anything about them. All I could think about was how much more they would grow in the next two months." She frowned and then added, "I guess the feed was better than I thought."

''Or the breed was different.''

''I, also, didn't realize that cattle were territorial,'' Clem commented.

''Not in the traditional sense of the word,'' Ryan answered, shooting a mischievous look at Dexter. ''It's more like each bull is trying to keep what's his, so he has to tag along to make sure the other bulls don't venture into his territory.''

Randy swatted at his brother, which Ryan ducked with a chuckle. Dexter changed the subject.

''How are your horses?'' he asked. His voice was all business and Clem appreciated his professionalism.

She sat down again.

''Not as fit as yours are,'' she said. ''Archie is the best of the bunch. He's got a lot of cow sense and he and I get along well.''

Ryan turned his head toward Dexter. ''It would be good to have a horse out there that knows where it's going.''

''He's very well trained and takes to strangers easily.''

Randy nodded before turning to Dexter. ''We'll need to see how they travel and check in on any favorite watering spots over the next day or so.'' To Clem, he added, ''Ryan has a way of knowing where cows want to hang out, where they're heading. He can even tell you what they've eaten last, and match it up with the feed from a particular area."

"I want to take a ride up this creek," Ryan said as he pushed his plate back and patted his tummy with satisfaction. "Is there a peak or two that would give me a good vantage point?"

Clem tapped three peaks. "You can get to those with a truck, in about forty minutes, but it's actually quicker by horse. It gets pretty steep. You can always tell where you are by where the reservoir is." She pointed to the big man-made lake. "Once you get to the top, you'll need to ride or walk down if you want a closer look."

Ryan exchanged glances with his brother. "Sounds good."

"How long do you think this phase will take?"

Ryan shrugged and gave her a broad smile. "Depends on the cows. They might like me enough to reveal themselves to me."

"A couple of days. We'll see," Randy assured her.

Ryan blotted his mouth with the napkin and looked at Clem as he stood up. "You cooked, point me to the kitchen and we'll clean up."

Clem protested. "No, no. You just relax. You've been driving all day. I've got it taken care of."

Randy brushed the biscuit crumbs off of his flat belly as he got up. "At least let us clear the table.

It's mostly our junk, anyway. Also, that dinner was excellent.''

Clem smiled. ''Thanks.''

''We love home cooking.''

''Good. I have a great menu planned for your entire stay. I'll also do all the laundry you need. I set out fresh linens in the bunkhouse for anyone who wants it—unless you'd rather stay in the house. There's plenty of room.''

Randy and Ryan exchanged a laugh. ''No, ma'am. We much prefer the bunkhouse. If you knew how we were raised, you'd understand.''

In quick time, the brothers had cleared the table, folded up the tablecloth and put away their maps. Then they grabbed their hats off the long pine bench next to the front door and tipped them toward Clementine. ''It's an early start tomorrow. We should be hitting the sack. Five a.m. comes awfully early.''

''Clem, thank you again for the delicious dinner,'' Ryan said. ''We'll see you then.''

Clem smiled. ''That you will. If you liked the dinner, you'll love what I've got planned for breakfast. Oh, by the way, which one of you wants to borrow Archie?''

She had a month's worth of backlogged correspondence to attend to and she had planned on a day of paperwork. This would be perfect because

Archie would get some well-deserved exercise and companionship.

"Borrow Archie?" Randy chuckled. "That's funny."

Ryan laughed. "We've got our own mounts. You'll be riding Archie."

"Me?" Clementine squeaked, and shook her head in protest. "No, I'll just get in the way. I'm sure that you all ride much faster and better than I do. I'll just slow you down."

"We promise we won't go too fast," Ryan said, winking at her. "Besides, I'm being purely selfish. You see, we're inherently lazy. Your knowledge is worth a fortune. See you bright and early."

"Coming, Dex?" Randy asked.

"In a minute," Dexter said. "There are a couple of things I'd like to discuss with Clem."

CHAPTER FOUR

THEY WERE ALONE and the house seemed cavernous to Clem. Dexter stayed seated, leaning back in his chair.

"I can't believe they want me to go with them tomorrow," she said with a small smile.

Dexter's face was pensive, then he cleared his throat. "It'll save us time," he acknowledged. "If it were up to me, though, I'd rather you stay home."

Stay home.

Those words brought back clear images of her father telling her to stay home during a rare lightning storm when the horses were going crazy. She'd been about fourteen at the time and knew the horses better than anyone. It had been one of the few times Jim Wells had ever raised his voice to her. She remembered seething, knowing she could help and feeling as if her father had just discounted her contribution to the ranch. Part of her realized that he'd been concerned about her safety, but the part of her that was still fourteen years old told her different.

"Really?" Clem experienced a small prick of annoyance. "And why exactly would that be?"

"Probably for the same reason you don't want to go." He leaned forward, hands on the back of the chair. "You'll be a lot safer right here than out there."

Clem felt her back straighten. How odd. Five minutes ago, she couldn't wait to give them this burden, now she was bristling.

Stay home.

"You sure you don't need me to go to this party with you?" Clem asked her husband.

Nick gave her a distracted smile, his fingers fumbling with his tie. Clem straightened it for him, her fingers lingering on his broad chest. Did he flinch or was that just her imagination?

She smiled up at him. "I can be ready in a jiffy. I can wear the sparkly black number you picked out in Las Vegas."

He shook his head. "No, no. You'll just be bored. You look tired. Why don't you just stay home and rest?"

Stay home.

She knew now that was the night her husband had begun his affair. Would her life have been different if she'd insisted on going? Or would she have simply put off the inevitable?

"Sometimes we can't always do the safe thing," she said, not able to keep the snap out of her voice.

Dexter sat a little straighter at her tone, but said nothing, just waited for her to finish her thought.

When she didn't, he pressed her. "Would you like to elaborate on that?"

She shrugged and walked to the kitchen, not wanting to look at him. It seemed as if he saw too much with those eyes. Forcing her voice to be light, she said over her shoulder, "You're here, aren't you?"

Dexter followed her.

Clem jerked up the faucet handle, running the water at full blast, checked to see if it was hot, then plugged the sink before she squirted a stream of dishwashing liquid into the basin.

"And?"

"You're retired, remember? Isn't it a lot safer to stay retired than come out here?"

"You don't know why I'm here." His voice was so quiet she turned down the faucet to hear him.

She pressed her lips together and then looked him straight in the eye. "I have a pretty good idea."

The corners of his mouth turned up, but the smile didn't make it to his eyes. "Really, now."

She nodded. "You're here to face whatever it was that made you retire in your prime."

The silence lasted so long Clem knew she'd

guessed right. *And you don't want to be lonely anymore.* But she wasn't going to add that. Maybe his friends had reminded him there was a lot more to life than existing. Dexter continued to say nothing. He just opened and closed the cabinet drawers.

''Looking for something?'' Clem asked.

He didn't respond but kept on with his methodical survey.

Clem sniffed. If he didn't want to talk, that was okay. Clem had plenty to keep her occupied, each dish getting special attention. She worked her way through the china and the silverware, stacking them on the dish drainer. When she turned to get the goblets, she was surprised to find Dexter pulling a couple of dish towels out of a drawer.

He plucked a plate off the dish drainer and dried it with efficient movements.

''It was nice of you to put out the good stuff,'' he said gruffly.

''My mother always did that when we had company.''

Another silence.

He broke it this time. ''The dinner was excellent.'' Clem could tell his compliment was sincere.

''Thank you.''

Long pause.

''Where do these go?'' Dexter asked. He had two cabinets open, searching for a similar china pattern.

"Oh, those go in the dining room. Just stack them up. I'll put them away later."

"Don't trust me, huh?" He gave her a real smile that transformed his whole face.

DEXTER MEANT IT AS A JOKE, but somehow his voice had taken on a much more serious tone.

Clem's eyes were enormous as she dried her hands on a towel, then picked up his stack of plates.

For once, he shifted uncomfortably. "You don't have to answer that."

She hugged the plates to her chest, her blue eyes never leaving his face. "I would trust you with my life."

The words hung in the air, and as if she was disturbed by her admission, she swept out of the kitchen.

Dexter swallowed hard. Why did even the simplest conversations with her have such an impact on him? Dex didn't know what hurt him the most—the complete trust in her eyes or the sad fact that her trust was misplaced. He couldn't save lives. He could barely live his own.

"I wouldn't go that far," he said, his voice strained, as he followed her into the dining room with the silverware.

She nodded. "I would."

They lapsed into silence again, and he held out

the forks and knives. She stared at them as if she didn't know what they were. Then, avoiding all contact, she took them from him and began arranging them in the top drawer of the china cabinet.

''Your mother didn't want the china?'' Dexter asked. He'd been impressed with the quiet opulence of the ranch house. It was as expansive as the Victorian was cloistered. The ranch house spoke of elegant holiday meals and happy family gatherings. It seemed far too big a place for Clementine to rattle around in by herself.

''Their new house is a lot smaller and my mother didn't want to take too much. As long as I'm staying here, it made sense for them to keep the bulky furniture here.''

''And your furniture and china?''

''My furniture and china?'' Clem straightened each plate in the cabinet so the designs were all in perfect alignment.

''You said you were married before.''

''Sold'' was all she said.

CLEM DIDN'T WANT TO BE RUDE, but Dexter was probing too deeply for comfort.

He seemed to be aware of that because he let the subject drop.

''I guess I should get going,'' he said, moving toward the door.

"You don't have to," Clem blurted as she watched him walk across the living room to retrieve his hat. "You could stay here."

He stopped still and Clem realized what that had sounded like.

"No, n-no. Not that." She waved her hands in the air and then dropped them at his inquiring look. She crossed over to the pine bench, wanting to explain that she'd just wanted to offer him the same thing she'd offered the Miller brothers—a bed in the house. Not *her* bed. The words, however, wouldn't come out.

DEXTER HAD ALWAYS THRIVED on the unknown, which was why he'd loved chasing feral cows and why he loved the challenge of working with difficult horses. But he was smart enough to know that if he was going to survive an encounter with the unknown, he'd better partner it with the familiar. Randy and Ryan Miller were familiar. They'd worked together so long that they could be a quarter mile away and still predict each other's movements, relying on hand signals, intuition and the actions of the cows they herded. That's what made them so good.

Dexter could sense the personalities of the cows, and they seemed to telegraph their movements, their intentions to him, which allowed him to direct a dog to watch those cattle that seemed restless or discontent. Some cowboys complained that his drives were boring because nothing happened; others said Dexter was the luckiest son of a gun who ever walked a cow trail. Dexter knew it wasn't about luck. Accidents didn't happen because he didn't let them happen.

Until Joanna died.

From that day on, his abilities and intuition had evaporated with the intensity of his grief. But now, three years later, he yearned for their return so he could read this woman who barely came up to his chin. His mouth went dry, and Dexter became acutely aware of how close she was standing to him, so close he could smell the shampoo in her hair. She looked up and then glanced away, but didn't move an inch.

"No. I don't think so." Each word was distinct. He studied every detail of her face, wanting desperately to take her up on her offer. Instead, he very carefully placed his hands on her shoulders.

Clem jumped at the warmth of his hands, the intimacy of his touch.

"So tense," Dexter murmured.

"I'm not tense." She shook her head for emphasis.

Those hands began to massage her shoulders, not sensuously, as she would have suspected, but clinically, therapeutically. She felt her knees give way as she closed her eyes and realized she was no better than Cowchip, falling victim to those lethal hands.

When the motion of his hands stopped, Clem remembered to open her eyes, and found his intense gaze on her face, but something in his green eyes changed as he looked at her mouth. His hands moved from her shoulders to the base of her neck, his fingers tangling in the fine hairs at her nape. Until that moment, Clem hadn't known how sensitive that part of her body was.

With his hands cupped around the back of her head, she stared up at him, at the sensual curve of his bottom lip, the slight cleft in his chin, the dark stubble. She could see his even teeth up close. She swallowed hard, mesmerized by the combination of the rhythmic caress of his hands and the fact that she was sure—just as she'd been sure she wanted him to come today—that he was going to kiss her.

She knew it.

And wanted it.

She closed her eyes and could feel the warmth of his breath fan her eyelashes. The back of his right hand stroked her temple, and she thought she was going to pass out if he didn't kiss her soon.

Then those magnificent hands were gone, leaving

her with only a slight flick on her nose. Her eyes popped open at the desertion.

"I think—" Dexter said, his voice low and husky, "I'd better sleep in the bunkhouse."

With a laugh, he jammed his hat on his head and was gone, moving quickly and silently for a man so large. Clem slid down the wall until she met the pine bench. Her head was suddenly dizzy, the blood having drained out of it to puddle at the soles of her feet.

Now, that was a cowboy.

BY THE TIME DAWN was breaking over the Sierras, Dexter sat on his favorite horse, Calisto, who was delicately working her way through the rough brush of the Diablo mountain range. Calisto was as moody as they came, but after fifteen years, Dexter would trust the horse with his life. Dexter would never take New Horse out for serious work. He just wasn't ready, though Dexter still had hope he would turn out to be a good cattle horse. After all, it seemed as if the best cattle horses were as crazy as their owners.

Not that there was any craziness to this ride. He felt as if he was out on a Sunday, just enjoying the view. He wasn't about to let Clementine near any danger, so they'd slowed the pace and picked her brain for all the information that she'd collected over the past year.

He would have preferred to explore on his own. By himself, Dexter would have taken a ride around the perimeter, poked around in different areas, maybe even spotted a few cows, which was the best way to find out how dispersed they actually were. He'd be ready to compare notes with Randy and Ryan when they returned from their own scouting trips. But with Clem riding along, they'd be lucky to get halfway before having to turn back. That wasn't Clementine's fault, Dexter allowed. She'd shown enough sense to know that she couldn't keep up.

Dexter heard Clementine's delighted laugh behind him and, against his will, looked over his shoulder. She had a cream felt Stetson pulled down over her face. At least it didn't look as new as she did. Randy and Ryan had slowed to walk with her.

Dexter ignored the twinge that he felt. He wasn't jealous or anything. He just didn't appreciate the way Randy watched her, almost as if he wanted to swallow her down in one go.

Well, Randy hadn't kissed her.

Dexter shook off that thought and wondered why he just didn't have the guts to walk away. Hell, he couldn't even stop himself from stealing another look at her. She was certainly a no-frills kind of rider, her saddle was plain but fit perfectly, and she sat on Archie as if she'd been born there.

But he was none too pleased with the way she smiled back at Randy.

Randy would be the worst thing for Clementine. He and Joanna had fit each other like milk and cookies, cake and frosting. But Clem needed someone different from Randy. She needed someone to protect her, keep her safe. Randy was the easygoing type. Whatever Joanna had wanted, Joanna got, even if it wasn't necessarily the best thing for her. Clem needed someone more like—himself.

He rolled the thought around in his mind.

She was a nice-looking woman, a little on the complicated side, but he kind of liked that about her. He couldn't suppress a chuckle. Clementine Wells had proved herself to be a bundle of contradictions, helpless and resourceful, uncertain and determined, soft and stubborn.

"There's one!" Clementine hissed as she reined Archie to a stop.

Randy halted Shuckabur right next to her, and they all turned to look in the direction she was pointing.

"I didn't think we'd find one this close to the ranch," Clem said with disgust. "It's mocking me." She shook her finger at it. "Well, I tell you, cow, I brought in the big guns, so enjoy your freedom. You'll be steak soon. Oh, there's another."

"Woooo-whee!" Ryan whistled through his teeth, then pushed his hat back so he could see better.

Dexter backed up Calisto several feet, for a better angle, his heart thumping with curious excitement. He scanned the area and spotted at least four more cows, peacefully grazing on the new grass. They were clearly marked with the Wells family brand—bright yellow tags in their ears.

The cows gave warning snorts, and Dex could feel Calisto go tense with anticipation. He tugged slightly on the reins to keep her from moving forward to investigate.

If anything, Clem had underestimated the size of the cattle. Dexter couldn't stop the satisfied smile that overtook him. It mirrored Randy's as he studied Clem's herd, almost pure white with small brown markings on the face and legs. Longhorn? He shook his head. It was impossible to tell what they were that far away. Dexter allowed Calisto to go a little closer.

The horn span wasn't four feet, like Clem'd said earlier, but at least five. And they weren't benign, either. They turned up and out, and even looked as if they'd been sharpened with some regularity. They could do some real damage to a horse and cowboy alike if the pair wasn't careful.

The nearest cow looked at them. Yes, there was some Longhorn. But there was something else that gave it a wily appearance. Massive chest, narrow, agile legs, skinny tail. Lots of lean muscle, not a lot of fat. A formidable opponent.

Something that might have been called fear, if he could remember what fear felt like, rippled through him. He sat up straighter, scanning the narrow sloping hills for signs of even more cows. His palms itched to get closer and he actually gripped his rope.

Calisto continued to move from hoof to hoof, a small dance of anticipation. It'd be foolish to try anything now. They didn't have the dogs. But he wanted to. He hadn't had a challenge like this in too long. These cows explained why no one else had taken this job. Clem had actually been able to get in several hundred of these? How had she done that with out-of-shape horses and untrained dogs? The experience would be fodder for conversation later on this evening.

For now he studied the biggest cow. It studied him back, apparently having dismissed Clem, Ryan and Randy as no threat.

You aren't so big, the cow telegraphed to him without a blink of its dark eyes. Then with the ease of a confident contender, the cow turned and walked away, tail twitching at something small and annoying.

Calisto neighed and skittered backward with excitement. Calisto definitely enjoyed her work, even sometimes to her own detriment.

Clem came up beside Dexter; Archie was perfectly comfortable with the terrain.

Her face was flushed and she looked thrilled. "Did you see them?"

"See what?"

"The cows." She clicked her tongue with impatience.

"Those things?" He tilted the brim of his hat in the general direction.

"Yes."

"Anomalies." That's what he wanted to think. It was better to believe that what he'd just seen was nothing more than a few strands of DNA gone astray.

Clem shook her head with great regret. "'Fraid not. Those are the midgets. Their bigger siblings are up the mountain a ways. These are the weaklings."

He swiveled his head to see if she was kidding.

She wasn't.

Her mouth turned down into a pensive scowl. "I marked the ones that we couldn't get in. See the red paint on the rear? That's me. He was a little critter three months ago."

"What do you have up there? Plutonium?"

Clem shook her head. "Don't know. There are power lines over that way. Don't know if that would make them radioactive. Especially when you consider my family's been putting out cows here for two generations. This is the first set that's grown so big. Maybe their water got an extra dose."

Dexter felt a new wave of respect for Clem. She was readily accepting the blame for her renegade cattle, admitting her inexperience, but the truth was even a very experienced rancher would have a heck of a time getting those beasts in. This didn't seem like Clem's fault at all. Calves pretty much looked alike. Who could know what they'd eventually grow into?

Randy rode up, still studying the cows. "Maybe they'll herd." But he didn't sound too convinced.

"They might," Dexter acknowledged.

Randy gave him a quick look. A wide grin lit up his face. "You want to try?"

It wasn't a dare, but it felt like one.

"The horses are dying for a workout," Ryan added.

"What about her?" Dexter angled his head toward Clem.

He could see her straighten in the saddle, her frown telling him what she thought about his words.

"Clem?" Randy addressed her.

"Yes?" She looked alert.

"Can you follow orders?" Randy asked. "I mean seriously follow orders."

"Yes," she answered.

"We want to see how easily they herd, so we're going to try these few out. We don't have the dogs..." Ryan's voice trailed off.

"So I'll be the dogs?" Clem looked at Randy and then shot a quick look at Dex.

Ryan grinned. "Not just you, but me, too."

Dexter edged Calisto forward. "No, Ryan, I'll do it. If Clem wants to go, I'll go with her."

"So, Clem, you up for a little excitement?" Randy asked.

Clem looked uncertain and Dexter didn't want to push her.

"If you don't want to, you don't have to. Ryan and I'll go and you can stay with Randy." Dexter meant the words to be supportive.

If anything, all they did was stiffen Clem's posture.

After a long pause she said in a firm voice, "I'll go."

"You should get to the other side and wait," Randy said to Dexter.

Dexter nodded. "We'll wait for your signal." He bestowed a rare smile on Clem. "You wanted some excitement. Looks like you're going to get it. We need to ride right up to them as quickly as we can and then start to make a lot of noise. But get out of the way fast.''

Clem nodded.

''Clem, go northwest, and Dex, you go northeast. See if you can turn them so they'll start running south. If they herd, our job is going to be a lot easier than we thought,'' Ryan said, his eyes never leaving the cows.

Clem could hardly breathe, her heart was beating so wildly. So this was what it was like to work with people who knew what they were doing. She directed Archie down the small incline, not daring to look at Dexter, who rode right next to her. Controlling her excitement, she reined Archie in the direction that Dexter sent her. When she was in position, she stopped and waited for Randy to wave his hat.

She thought she could see excitement in Dexter Scott's eyes, and Clem suddenly realized that Dexter needed to prove something as much as she did. He looked at her and nodded. They were equals now, and Clem felt a burst of joy. Then the signal came and she hunkered down over Archie and let him go.

AS HE URGED CALISTO FORWARD Dexter watched Clem ride straight toward him, her body low, her legs in perfect position. She spurred Archie faster, a grin plastered on her face, then cut left at the same moment he cut right, and as they rode side by side, something inside of him burst open. Life didn't get any better than this.

When he increased his speed, she stayed right with him effortlessly. Then as if reading each other's minds, they both began to whoop. Dexter watched the cows startle, then scatter, only to organize a little farther down, at which point Randy and Ryan took off after them, trying to turn them. In a perfectly synchronized move, the cattle swerved left, and then right, all at a dead run.

Dexter allowed Calisto to join the fun as he followed the cows, determined to figure out every trick they had. These critters were speedy and used to running. They could easily stampede if there were too many of them. So Dexter made a mental note to keep their number low—groups of fifteen to twenty, and no more—while moving them from one corral to the next.

After about fifteen minutes, he signaled the Miller brothers and they dropped off, letting the cows disappear into the brush.

Clem came riding up, her face flushed with excitement, her breathing hard. "Gosh, that was fun."

Dexter could barely look at Clem, she was so beautiful. Her eyes sparkled, and her I'm-not-too-sure-what-I'm-doing veneer had slipped just a little with her exertion.

Randy reined Shuckabur right next to them and grinned with great optimism. "They turned really easy."

"Skittish, though," Ryan put in. "They'd be prone to stampeding, don't you think?"

Dexter nodded. "Small groups."

"That's what I was thinking. Fifteen or twenty."

"Maybe ten to start with, just so we know what we're dealing with. Once we get a little experience with them, we can move a whole group," Randy suggested.

Dexter understood his point. He turned to Clem, whose cheeks were still bright pink with her effort. "You said these were small?" he asked. He didn't mean to be skeptical, but he'd been around a lot of cattle and they didn't come much bigger than these.

She nodded. "Yes. There are some bigger ones up the mountain, where we lost them. We didn't do any trial runs."

"Our form of research," Randy said. He nodded to Clem. "You did great out there."

Dexter watched Clem smile at Randy's compliment and kicked himself for not complimenting her first.

"So where does this road go?" Dexter indicated

the small truck path as his eyes settled on Clem. She was still beaming.

''Up, around and back to the ranch,'' Clem replied. She pointed and Dexter's eyes were drawn to the slender curve of her forearm. He'd felt those arms wrapped around his neck. ''This cuts north, the other trail we were on goes south. That road will put you out by the corral, this will put you by the bunkhouse.''

Dexter nodded to Randy. ''Which one do you want?''

''Road or partner?''

''Road. You and Ryan go one way, we'll go the other.''

''You sure?'' Randy raised an eyebrow. ''If you want to go it alone, we'll take her—don't mind having Clem along.''

Dexter minded Randy having Clem along.

He minded a lot.

''Nah.'' He shook his head. ''I'm up for a little baby-sitting.''

CHAPTER FIVE

CLEMENTINE STIFFENED AT Dexter's words, then almost lost her seat on Archie, she was so startled by a swift wink Dexter sent her way. It was a private, intimate wink she was positive neither Randy nor Ryan saw. In fact, he'd delivered it with such stealth she wasn't certain she'd seen it. But then she noticed the twinkle in his eyes. Lord above. Dexter Scott was devastating when he was relaxed. Twice as dangerous as usual.

"There's some information I'd like from Clem, anyway," Dexter said as he straightened up.

"Okay." Randy met Dex's eyes, and then cleared his throat. "Ryan and I'll go that way. Meet you back at the main house."

Clem watched Randy and Ryan take the north trail. She and Dexter continued in their original direction. She'd already become accustomed to Dexter Scott's lack of chatter, but she didn't expect to ride in complete silence. After fifteen minutes, she ventured, "Don't know how much I know."

"What?" Dexter regarded her seriously.

"You said you wanted some specific information from me," she said. She found herself gesturing with the reins and dropped her hands. "You said that to Randy."

"Ahh." He nodded but didn't say anything else.

They rode some more, the horses content at a slow walk.

"Pretty country," he commented.

"I like it," she replied. "It's different from the desert." Then she added. "I like the desert, too."

"I don't know if I so much like the desert. It's where I ended up. I didn't exactly choose it."

That observation surprised Clementine. She'd assumed he had. She'd figured he'd traveled all over the West and settled in the place he liked best. Each small piece of information she learned added yet another facet to him. He had a reason for coming out of retirement and he didn't choose to live in the desert. She wanted to probe him for more.

Instead, she said nothing, and for a while they just rode, their horses in perfect step.

"Seems like it'd be easier than this," he commented.

"What?" Clem asked.

"Getting to know someone."

Clem's mouth went dry and the joke she'd meant to utter got stuck in her throat. Did he want to get to know her better?

"Yes, I do," he said.

"Would you stop doing that?" Clem was disconcerted by the steadiness of his gaze on her face.

"Doing what?"

"Answering questions I never ask."

"You ask them."

"No, I don't."

"Yes, you do," he contradicted her. He reached out to touch her cheek. "You're easy."

"Easy?" Clem didn't know whether to be pleased or offended.

"To read. Your face tells me everything I need to know."

"Like what? What question do I have?"

"Whether or not I have designs on you. If that's the reason I didn't want you to go with Randy and Ryan."

"And do you?" She was trying to make her voice light, flirtatious even, but it came out uncertain.

He took a deep breath and said, "Yes," before he spurred Calisto forward. "I do need to know a few things, though."

"Such as?" Clem gladly accepted the change in subject. If they talked about cows, she didn't have to notice how his hands rested on his thighs when he rode or how straight he sat or that he'd admitted he had designs on her.

"Why was it so important for you to run the ranch?"

She swallowed but didn't reply.

"How much did it have to do with your divorce?"

She didn't know what to say. How could she tell him everything and nothing? Yes, the divorce had caused the upheaval that had led her back to her parents' ranch, but running the ranch had more to do with something she'd been missing long before the divorce.

"Sorry," he said. "I didn't mean to pry."

Instead of answering, Clem plunged in with a request of her own. "Tell me first why you decided to retire."

DEXTER COULDN'T BEAR to look at Clementine. Her eyes were so compassionate.

"I had a sister." He could barely say the words. She didn't say anything, just listened.

"You ride like her. She was very good. She, Randy, Ryan, my good friend Ben Thorton and I did everything together. We roped cows, we traveled together. She and Randy were getting close."

"What happened to her?"

"She was killed in an accident."

He saw that Clementine paled as she processed that bit of information.

"I'm sorry."

"Me, too."

"And you feel responsible for her death? That's why you quit?"

Such a simple question with such a complicated answer. Dexter'd forgotten that getting to know someone meant treading into murky, emotional areas that sometimes were better left alone.

"It's not that I feel responsible for her death." He tried to explain, but words eluded him. He *was* responsible for her death. If he had said no, Joanna would never have gone with them. She would have stayed home. If he had said no, she and Randy would be married and they'd have a passel of kids. To Clem, he said, "She was a very independent girl. That's what killed her. She'd have been better off if she'd stuck closer to home."

"But maybe that wasn't what she wanted to do," Clem said, her voice thoughtful. "Maybe the furthest thing from her mind was staying home."

"Maybe," he acknowledged. Clem didn't say anything that hadn't been said to him before, but it didn't make him feel better. It didn't make him miss Joanna any less.

"You can't blame yourself for something you couldn't help." She touched his arm. "Accidents happen. She'd probably be mad at you for trying to take responsibility."

He didn't comment, his attention caught by something in his peripheral vision.

CLEM WATCHED DEXTER. Apparently there were things Dexter Scott didn't want to talk about, either. He'd revealed very little, but she was sure that underneath his stoic exterior there was a cauldron of feelings that he couldn't express. But she also knew that the more she pressed him, the more he would slip though her fingers.

"What is it?" she asked.

"Shh." Dexter had lowered his voice to a whisper. "Right behind us."

Clem peeked over her shoulder, and sure enough two glittering eyes stared at her.

"It's as if she's tracking us," Clem said with a shiver.

"Not likely. Cows are prey animals. They don't track."

"Let's walk forward and see what she does," Clem suggested. "Then we can tell what she's doing."

They walked about two hundred feet and heard wary rustling behind them.

Clem looked back over her shoulder. "She's following us. This happened last time."

"What happened?"

"One charged me."

"This one?"

Clem looked carefully. "Don't know. Could be. All I know is it scared the pants off me."

"Let's see what it does when it's confronted," Dexter said, turning Calisto. "Stay put."

"What are you going to do?"

"Research," he said, before spurring Calisto to a full run.

Clem watched in horror and fascination as Dexter played a particularly dangerous game of chicken. With a cow that was up for the challenge. Like a bull, she bent her head, showed her large, pointed horns to advantage and charged. Dexter and Calisto veered at the last possible moment, Dexter's leg coming close to her lethal horn.

Clem was so intent on making sure Dexter was all right, she didn't realize that the cow was heading straight at her.

"Get out of there!" Dexter hollered.

His words jerked her into motion and she spun Archie, who needed no more urging to get out of the way.

"Go down the path," Dexter directed.

Clem did what she was told, not looking back. She could hear the pounding of the hooves behind her, getting closer and closer. Or maybe that was just her heart. This was precisely why she'd wanted to do paperwork today. She didn't *enjoy* being chased by cows.

There was a bellow of fury behind her and she jerked to a stop when she figured out the cow was no longer chasing her. Unbelievable. Dexter had roped the cow around her horns and he and Calisto were pulling her toward a grove of trees, away from Clem.

The cow was not going without a fight, though, a noisy, roaring fight. Clem sat helpless, her heart pounding hard. What could she do to help? Her mind went blank.

She was close to crying with the frustration of watching and not being able to do anything. Dexter's mouth was set in a grim line and his eyes were narrowed as he and Calisto dragged the cow toward the trees, inch by painful inch, the muscles bulging in Calisto's legs as she resisted the angry pull of the cow. Clem crossed her fingers, hoping the cow would tire itself out soon. However, the loud snorting of the animal made her think it wasn't going to happen. The cow was mad.

And clever.

With no warning, it changed directions, crossing under Calisto. Clem screamed when she saw that the rope held taut by Dexter was about to be wrapped around Calisto's neck. Without thinking, she spurred Archie toward Calisto, pulling out a small hunting knife from a pocket in her saddle. Inches away from the other horse, she hooked her foot in her stirrup and leaned over as far as she could to slice through Dexter's rope.

The force of the rope's splitting sent them all flying. Within seconds the cow bellowed and took off through the trees.

"Damn!" Dexter was on his feet in an instant. "What the hell did you think you were doing? You didn't have to cut the line."

He stood towering over her. He extended his hand and Clem almost refused to take it. Almost. He hauled her to her feet.

"You okay?" he asked, his voice gentling.

"I'm fine. And you don't have to swear at me," Clem said as she brushed herself off. She looked around to find Archie and Calisto waiting patiently.

He looked at her in surprise, his voice mild. "I wasn't swearing at you."

"It sounded like you were." Clem searched for her hat, seeing it a few yards away. She mimicked him, "What the hell did you think you were doing?"

He stared hard at her, uncomprehending.

"What's that, if it's not swearing?" She couldn't help the primness that had entered her voice. It masked the terror that had seized her when she'd thought Calisto was going to be beheaded before her eyes.

"If you're going to hang around with us," Dexter

said, his tone measured, "you'll have to grow a slightly thicker skin."

"Or maybe you shouldn't yell at me."

He cocked his head to the side as if he were trying to puzzle her out, much the way Cowchip did when she was telling the dog something. It was the look that said *I know what she's saying is important, but I'm not exactly sure what she means.*

"If whatever I said hurt your feelings, then that's something you'll have to get over," Dexter informed her, and then added, his voice clipped, "It's not all about you."

If her feelings weren't hurt before, those words finished the job. Clem felt as if he'd just slapped her. Without replying, she mounted Archie and took off in the direction of the house. Dexter wasn't far behind, Calisto easily keeping up with Archie's trot.

They rode that way for a long while, the tension between them remaining despite the beautiful scenery surrounding them. Clem sucked in some deep breaths, trying to regain control of herself. She'd overreacted. She knew that. But she still wanted him to hug her and tell her that she'd done a good job.

It's not all about you. Those words stuck in her mind, poking at her sense of herself. Of course, it wasn't about her. She knew that, too.

"I'm sorry if your feelings are hurt," Dexter ventured after a while.

She couldn't look at him.

"You could at least thank me," she said, her voice clipped.

"Thank you?" Dexter asked, puzzled.

"Yes."

"Okay. Thank you."

"You're welcome." She felt slightly better.

There was another long minute.

He cleared his throat. "Exactly what am I thanking you for?"

Irritation ballooned inside Clementine. She stared at him. "You really don't know, do you?"

"No, ma'am."

"I saved your horse."

"Okay." It was almost as if she could see Dexter's mind processing her words. He finally said, "So how exactly did you save 'Listo?"

"I kept her from being garroted. Surely you realize the rope would have cut off her head."

"Of course." He nodded.

They rode another hundred yards in silence.

Finally, Clem sneaked a glance in his direction and to her exasperation she saw that rare smile playing at the sides of his mouth.

DEXTER TRIED TO HOLD BACK his amusement, but it was hard not to laugh at her grim expression. She was really too serious. His own pulse had calmed now that the incident was over. The truth was that he'd had every intention of cutting the cow loose. Given the location, he hadn't believed he could tie it down, especially when he saw how much it fought.

But she couldn't have known that. She could only go by what she saw. There'd been panic in her eyes when she'd ridden at them, the knife clutched in her hand. If he hadn't sliced the rope first, she would have probably gotten a good portion of his and Calisto's leg. He supposed that he had sworn at her, but from the way her hand had been trembling when he'd helped her to her feet, he knew she was deeply shaken and that it was just as well for her to direct her fright at him and his perceived insult. If she was mad about something as trivial as swearing, she wouldn't be thinking about how terrifying these cows of hers were.

He would have to have some long discussions with Randy and Ryan. If this temperament was what they could expect in the others, then they would have to rethink how they were going to herd them. It also meant they'd have to do something about strays—any cows they couldn't get in would pose a great threat to Clem's future herds.

"What's so funny?" Clem asked, stopping his thoughts.

He shook his head. "Nothing."

"You're laughing at me." Her voice was accusing.

"No." He stared at her, his expression sobering. "I am very impressed with you and the fact you were able to get over half your herd in."

She met his gaze warily, then said, "It took me all summer and then some."

"You should have called for help earlier."

A glove hit him in the face. He caught it automatically.

She scowled at him, taking off her other glove, prepared to whack him with it.

He held up his hands with a defensive gesture. "Whoa. What did I say?"

"Why don't you listen to what I've said? I *tried* to get help. I called lots of cowboys and no one would take this on. Except you."

"Then you should have called me earlier."

She puffed out her cheeks. "Like you're listed in the phone book. Do you know how hard you were to track down?"

"I didn't want to be found."

"Obviously. I went through a lot."

"Yet, you found me." He held out her glove to her.

SOME QUALITY IN HIS VOICE changed, and Clem wasn't sure what to make of it.

"I had to," she said as she took the glove from him. "I just knew you could help me."

"How'd you know that?"

She shook her head. "I guess when the other outfits called you crazy, I knew I needed someone crazy."

His lips twisted into a smile. "I guess you could call me that."

Then, just as quickly as he'd opened up, Dexter Scott shut down. "Race you to the barn," he called as he pushed Calisto into a faster trot and took off.

Clem laughed in exasperation and followed. She leaned across Archie's neck and encouraged the horse to run as fast as he could. He responded, and soon the horses were side by side, their hooves thundering. Clem continued to whisper to Archie, and just as they reached the barn, Archie swept past Calisto. Clem screamed in celebration, her whooping startling the horses in the corral.

Dexter reined in Calisto, and they trotted around the courtyard to cool the horses down.

"You can ride," Dexter said, his eyes filled with the same joy she felt.

Out of breath, the thrill of racing still coursing through her, Clem basked in his admiration. "Yes."

"How long?"

''Ever since I could sit up,'' she said, her voice feeling light. *She* felt light, flippant. ''No, not really, but I don't remember learning how to ride. I've always ridden, and I've had Archie a long time. I just don't know cows.''

Dexter nodded. ''But you will. You just need practice. You did good out there. Kept your head.''

She slid off Archie and began to walk him around the courtyard. ''That's a first.'' She laughed wryly. How many times had her ex-husband accused her of being terrible in a crisis? ''My ex never thought so.''

''He must not have known you very well.''

The statement was too simple to be profound, but suddenly Clementine felt an overwhelming urge to cry. She stared at the cowboy who was dismounting next to her. How was he able to verbalize what she never even dared? How was it that she'd married a man who'd never really known her, had never even tried? *It's not all about you.* Dexter's words reverberated in her head. He was absolutely right. And that thought was simultaneously liberating and frightening.

She swallowed hard and walked faster. She needed time alone to process what Dexter had just shown her. All the anxiety of this afternoon, the exhilarating highs and the terrifying lows, had accumulated in the back of her throat.

"What?" he asked. "What's wrong? Did I say something wrong again?"

She shook her head. "No."

"You're not going to cry or something, are you?"

He sounded so uncertain she had to laugh. Here was a man who fearlessly wrestled feral cows for a living and yet seemed to dread little tears.

"Do you mind?"

"No. Not at all," he said quickly, keeping stride with her.

He was blurry because of the tears, but she smiled. "Liar."

"Sorry. Can I do anything?" he asked her in a practical voice.

The tears spilled over. She was caught between tears and laughter. "I-it's not something you need to fix. These are good tears. They'll pass."

"But you look awful." Dexter tilted up her chin and studied her face. "Your eyes are puffy, your nose is red. You need this." He handed her his handkerchief. "You need to blow your nose."

She grimaced and took the hankie before turning her back to blow her nose.

"So can you talk about what caused all this?"

She shrugged. With the hankie bunched in her hand, she started to unsaddle Archie.

"Let me," he said. In a few quick movements

he'd untied her knots and pulled the saddle off. "You're incapacitated."

"Crying doesn't make you incapacitated," Clem protested. "It's just crying. It's releasing emotion. It's a good thing. Didn't you cry when your sister died?"

Dexter's face closed. He yanked the saddle off Calisto and began to brush her vigorously.

Clem stopped sniffling and stared at him. "You cried for your sister, didn't you?" she asked again softly.

"This afternoon, we're going to ride higher into the mountains. I think it would be a good idea if you stayed home."

Clem could feel the pain and grief emanate from him. "Crying really is a good thing," she repeated.

"Why don't you go into the house? You look beat," Dexter suggested, his voice clipped. "I'll take care of Archie."

He'd shut down again, and Clem wished there was something she could do to help him release the pain. She couldn't imagine bottling up all the emotion, all the grief. It explained a lot about Dexter Scott, but it didn't make it clear why she needed to stay home when they went out this afternoon. If they were going up higher, they'd need her even more. She'd been exploring the mountains since she'd been allowed to ride alone. She had a superb sense of direction. However, judging from Dexter's erect posture and the force with which he brushed Calisto, Clem didn't think this was the time to try to convince him. With a peculiar sense of sadness, she walked back to the house.

DURING LUNCH, Randy, Ryan and Dexter talked cows. They compared notes and all came to the conclusion that they needed to check out the higher ground.

"We scoped the whole valley, and we only saw the odd one or two. There's not six hundred down here," Randy said. He scooped up more potato salad.

Clem was glad that he and Ryan were eating, because Dexter didn't touch a morsel. He thanked her when she gave him a plate containing a roast beef sandwich and then put it aside.

"I know there's a pocket of them somewhere," Ryan said.

"How far could they go?" Clem asked.

"Pretty far," Randy said. "They'd follow either water or feed. So if you've got some small trickles in the mountains, they might be there. Or maybe they found themselves a watering hole."

"That'd make our job easier."

"Except," Clem put in, "once you find them, you'll need to get them down."

Ryan laughed. ''We'll worry about that once—if we find them.''

''Ready?'' Dexter pushed back his chair. ''We've only got about five hours of daylight. I don't want to be caught in the dark.''

''I know my way around,'' Clem hinted.

''Yes.'' Randy shoveled the rest of the potato salad in his mouth. ''Let's go.''

Dexter addressed Clem without looking at her as he put his hat on, ignoring her hint. ''We'll be back before dark.''

''You don't need a guide?'' Clem asked more directly.

Randy started to nod, then Dexter cut him off. ''No. We're going to need to go a lot faster than we did this morning. You don't want to push Archie too much. We're taking fresh horses.''

''Okay.'' She did have that correspondence to do, but she still felt left out.

''It's just a quick trip,'' Ryan assured her. ''You'll be included when we get to the fun part.''

''Also, how many hands can you round up within the next three days?'' Dexter asked.

''How many will you need?''

''Five or six would be good. Tell them the pay's good.''

Clem gulped. ''I don't think I can come up with wages for six.''

"I've got it," Dexter said, clipped. "You just get them lined up. If we find the cows, we'll want to get going right away."

Without you was left unsaid, leaving Clem with the urge to salute him as he walked out.

THE AFTERNOON WENT QUICKLY. Clem spent most of her time on the phone, either pleading for more time on payments or trying to recruit cowboys. With each phone conversation, she stretched her father's credibility just that much further. Most everyone in the surrounding community knew about the fiasco with the cows, which seemed to make them cluck at her sympathetically. In the end, she could only rustle up two definite yeses, two maybes—depending on when they were needed—and six nos. She went through her father's Rolodex three times, looking at all of his cryptic notes, hoping for an odd phone number that would lead her to another hand. But it was late in the season and most cowboys had already booked with other ranches for branding, something Clem wouldn't be doing this season.

Clem shuffled the papers around her father's desk, a monstrous piece of walnut, and tried to push aside the feelings that she should be riding with Dexter, Randy and Ryan. She resented the fact that Dexter was as changeable as the weather and that his work and private life were so deeply entwined—

as she'd discovered the hard way while treading through his private life.

She ran her hands over the finely sanded wood of her father's desk, feeling like a fraud. The leather wing chair dwarfed her. The seat Jim Wells had left was, literally and metaphorically, a big one. If it hadn't been for her mother, she wouldn't have been trying to fill it. And she wasn't sure if that was a good thing.

She inhaled deeply. Family legends had it that Clem had been born on the desk, after a storm had kept Claire and Jim from getting to the hospital. In fact, her father loved to tell visitors that the deep marks on either side of the desk had been made by Claire during the contractions, although a truer explanation was probably that they were old bear markings on the original tree.

There was so much history to this desk, to this ranch. Coming back to run it had not been only a financial necessity, but a personal one, as well. Clem closed her eyes tight and wished for two miracles—one to erase the dismal numbers in front of her, and the other to give her just the smallest glimpse of her true self. She opened her eyes and still saw two months of unpaid bills. She talked to her father regularly, but she hadn't divulged the full extent of the problem. He knew she hadn't got the whole herd in, though the nine hundred she'd brought in had carried her through the summer.

"You know, honey, if this is too much, I can come back and help."

Clem had seen the concern in her father's eyes, but she'd just shaken her head. "No, Dad. I bought the cows. I'll figure it out."

"I just hope you know we don't mind helping."

Clem knew that, and in some ways it was the worst thing for her. She didn't want to always fly with a safety net. For once, she wanted to do a job on her own.

Her father continued. "I know you and your mother have talked, and your mother really wants to give you this time, but remember, it's not a sign of weakness to ask for help."

Clem knew that. *It's not all about you.* Dexter's words came back to her in full force. That was the problem. It'd always been about her. Her parents hadn't sold their ranch *for her.* Everything that her parents had done had been *for her.* Clem clenched her fist. Since people—namely, her father, her mother and her ex-husband—had always *done* for her, she'd never really known how to fend for herself. Worse, she wasn't sure she could. The realization made her stomach roll.

You'll have to grow a slightly thicker skin.

Clem jumped up and walked to the kitchen, disturbed to find that her thoughts were following her around. She plucked two chickens out of the refrigerator and carried them over to the sink. She rinsed the chicken, watching the pink juice swirl down the drain. She hated the fact that Dexter was right. It wasn't about her, and at the same time, it was.

She rubbed thyme, garlic, salt and paprika into the skin and then placed the two birds on a roaster and popped it into the oven. While the chickens cooked, she made three batches of corn bread. She saw how quickly the two batches of biscuits had disappeared the night before. Then she made a green salad, steamed broccoli and whipped up a batch of au gratin potatoes. When she saw she had more time, she made an apple pie. She was sweating by the end, but she felt purged and strong. She knew what she needed to do.

CHAPTER SIX

THE BACK DOOR OPENED just as Clem was pulling the chickens, perfectly basted and browned, out of the oven. She looked over her shoulder to see all three men walk in, talking and laughing.

"Good news, I hope," she said.

"Almost good news," Ryan countered. He had the maps rolled up under his arm.

"You found the cows?"

"We found evidence of the cows. So we know they're around and we know that they're close," Randy said. He leaned over her to take a big sniff of the chicken. "That smells great. I'm starved."

"It'll be about twenty minutes before the rest of the corn bread is finished baking, but you guys can start on this."

"Take your time," Ryan said.

Dexter had stayed conspicuously quiet.

"Did you find what you thought you would?" Clem asked him.

"Yeah, sure." His glance flickered over her and she felt dismissed.

She reminded herself that it wasn't all about her and she felt considerably better.

When she served the last of the corn bread, she smiled at the empty carcasses, the depleted salad bowl, two miserable stalks of broccoli and the crust around the au gratin bowl.

"We made you a plate," Ryan reassured her. "When Randy went back for thirds, Dex thought it would be a good idea if our hostess didn't starve while cooking for us."

"Thank you." She directed her comment to Dexter, who nodded briefly, as she sat down. It was a generous plate, heaped with chicken, both light and dark meat, potatoes and salad pieces falling off the plate.

A moment later, the maps were spread out, and Ryan started to put crosses by places where one or two cows had been spotted, circles where there were smaller herds in groups of ten to fifteen.

"We found fecal evidence— Sorry, Clem," Ryan apologized over his shoulder. "You're still eating."

"That's okay." Undaunted, she continued to chew.

"We found evidence of more than two hundred right here." Randy made a square right on the edge of one of the twin peaks.

Clem's eyes widened. "They made it that far?"

Ryan nodded. ''Any farther and they'd be working their way over the other side of the mountain. Some rancher on that end would be mighty happy.''

''How'd you do with the extra men?'' Dexter asked.

It was the first real remark he'd addressed to her.

''Not as well as I hoped.''

Three pairs of eyes were trained on her.

''What's not as well as you hoped?'' Randy asked.

''I have two for sures, two maybes, and lots of nos. It's a busy time of year.''

''Can we do it with only two more?'' Randy looked from his brother to Dexter.

Ryan nodded slowly. ''We'd have to plan differently. But we could do it. If they had good horses.''

''Anyway, you'd have at least three,'' Clem said.

''I thought you said just two were yeses,'' Randy said, his brow furrowing.

''I make three.''

''No!'' shot out of Dexter's mouth so fast that all eyes turned on him.

''Don't even think about it,'' Dexter said with a scowl so fierce that if Clem hadn't known better she would have been inclined to think that the response was out of proportion with the request.

''I wasn't 'thinking,''' Clem insisted before

Randy and Ryan could say anything. "I *am* going to ride with you."

"We can talk about it later, Clem," Randy said, trying to smooth over the tension that had filled the room.

"We do need a good guide. It'd sure be a lot easier if we had someone who knew where she was going. Clem might know a few shortcuts that will save hours," Ryan ventured, his manner business-like.

Clem reeled from the force of the fear in Dexter's eyes. Randy, however, seemed encouraged, though by what, Clem had no idea. Maybe it was the fact that Dexter's scowl had turned into a glower.

Randy backed up Ryan. "If she came for the pre-lims, then once the hard stuff starts, she could keep the corrals and the walkie-talkie. We could use a good point man, er, point woman there. That'd free up a man for the other stuff."

Ryan nodded. "That's a great idea."

"No!" burst out of Clem.

Randy's generally lighthearted gaze turned seri-ous as he looked at Clem. She read his message loud and clear. *If you want to go just shut up and let me do the talking.* But Clem wasn't about to let anyone do the talking for her, no matter how well-meant.

"I'm not going to sit back while you do all the

hard work,'' Clem clarified. She'd never been so assertive about anything in her life. Even when her marriage was falling apart she hadn't fought for it. Would the end have been different if she'd refused to let go when Nick had wanted out? She took a deep breath and said calmly, ''From now on, I'm going to be riding with you.''

''I said no.'' Dexter seemed to have recovered his sense of humor. He rearranged his facial features and gave her a smile, one that didn't reach his eyes. It was as if he didn't expect her to realize that a mouth turned up at the corners wasn't necessarily a smile. Maybe he thought a fake smile would soften the blow. He was mistaken.

Clem's eyes met his, and she saw a steel in there. She felt her inner strength waver. Was she crazy? It would be so much easier to stay home. But the more he protested, the more she knew she needed to go. Deep inside her, she realized that his objections probably had more to do with his sister than her.

''This is not a request,'' Clem said, her voice flat. ''This is my ranch.''

Dexter regarded her seriously for a full minute, then said, ''I won't be putting anyone at risk trying to save your skin.''

''I can look after my own skin, thank you very

much. Besides, there's not enough time for you all to wander around for weeks on end.''

''If we 'wander' around for weeks on end, it will be because of your poor judgment in choosing cattle. Remember—*we're* doing you the favor. If you don't want it, just say so and we'll be on our way tomorrow.''

DEXTER DIDN'T MEAN TO SOUND so blunt. His disagreement with her should have been settled privately. To shut himself up, he clenched his jaw and turned his attention away from Clem, who looked angry enough to pop the top of her skull off.

What in fool's name was that woman thinking?

There was no way he'd let her go. Only an idiot would make the same mistake twice. No one was going to pull her limp, lifeless body out of a gorge. He'd watched that once before and he wasn't about to repeat the experience. He'd tried to stop thinking about that before he remembered another face, a face he'd never cried for. An elfin face sporting a gutsy smile and a devil-may-care attitude—an attitude that had taken her right over the edge of a mountain. If the fall hadn't killed her instantly, she would have been irreparably damaged, probably paralyzed. In some ways what happened was for the best.

That's what everyone had told him.

They'd also told him it wasn't his fault. She'd died doing what she loved. Then they'd said they wished that when their time came, it would be over as quickly. That somehow didn't make him feel better. Or ease the gnawing guilt that permeated every moment of his day.

He could have stopped Joanna, but he hadn't.

He'd wanted his sister to have everything and could deny her nothing. Not even when she'd pleaded to go with him to look for a particularly stubborn bull. With Randy, Ryan and Ben riding shotgun, he hadn't wanted to say no. It was only after that he'd realized if he had said no, he wouldn't have had to watch Randy carry Joanna's broken body out of the gorge. He wouldn't have had to see the pain on Randy's face. Randy and Joanna had made no formal promises to each other, but Ryan had told Dex that after the funeral Randy had returned their grandmother's ring to the family vault.

"You're right," Clem said loudly.

Dexter pulled his attention back to Clementine, grateful for the distraction. Randy thought with that shade of hair, defiant tilt to the chin, and similar smile, Clem resembled Joanna. But to Dexter, those resemblances were superficial, where it counted, the two women were different. Joanna had been able to take care of herself. He knew because he'd spent most of his life teaching her how. It was the only way he could make sure she didn't have to depend on anyone. He'd wanted Joanna to choose to be in a good relationship and not be forced to stay with a man who didn't love her. Clem had spent her entire life depending on other people, and he didn't want to be next in line.

"You may be right," Clem repeated, the volume of her voice rising as if she thought the louder she talked the more convincing she would sound. Her fingers fiddled with her locket, belying the authority of her words. "It was my mistake for getting greedy," she admitted. "Choosing those cows was a stupid greenhorn mistake. There, I said it. Now, let's get past that and talk business."

"You can help us, just by getting us here," Ryan agreed, and Dexter saw him give her a signal with his eyes. "We'll take over from there. Hell, we're crazy enough as it is. No need for this to be contagious."

"Just for the ride around," Randy said, his voice sober and reasonable, too reasonable. Dexter shot him a warning look. Why would Randy persist? He'd suffered, too, when Joanna had died.

Randy met his stare with a direct one of his own. He continued, "It wouldn't hurt. Clem could give us some idea of where to set up the pens."

Didn't Randy remember finding her body?

"No." Dexter turned his head, cutting off the rest of the conversation.

Not very effectively, though, because Clem said, her chin high, in what was becoming a familiar gesture, "It wouldn't just be for the ride in. I already brought in half the herd with only a couple of part-time hands."

As the silence lengthened, Dexter became very aware of the fact the Miller brothers were now content to wait and watch.

"And almost killed yourself doing it." Dexter couldn't stop the bleakness from entering his tone as he took a guess. He knew he'd scored a direct hit when she reddened and looked away.

"There's no more discussion. If you want to go, you'll be going without me." He'd had enough, so he got up, being sure to handle the china with care despite his irritation.

"No!" Clem's voice rang with authority. "That's not acceptable."

"What did you say?" He could barely hear his own voice because blood pounded through his head so loudly.

She leaned toward him, her hands on her hips. "I said 'no' was *not* an acceptable answer. I don't know what's bugging you. But like you said earlier, it doesn't all have to do with me. I think this is about your sister."

Turnabout was apparently not fair play. She nailed his sore points just as easily as he'd hit hers.

"I need air" was all he could think to say. Then he grabbed his hat and left.

CLEM LOOKED AT THE MILLER brothers and gave them a rueful smile. "There's apple pie for dessert."

"I'm going to talk to him." Randy got up, his normally genial demeanor dark. "You have the dishes, Ryan?"

Ryan nodded.

Clem said, "Don't worry about the dishes. I'll do them." She lifted her plate and found that her hand was shaking. For someone who she hated conflict, she seemed awfully eager to jump in every chance she got.

"You're not used to asserting yourself," Ryan observed as he took the plate from her.

"Is it so obvious?" Clem really wanted to know; in fact, it felt as if her insides were burning to know. With steadier hands, she picked up the salad bowl and filled it with the broccoli plate along with the gratin dish. She followed Ryan into the kitchen.

After setting down his load of dishes, Ryan reached out to lift her locket and examine it. "Nice."

"My parents gave it to me for my sixteenth birthday."

"Joanna had one like it."

"Joanna?"

"Dexter's kid sister."

"The one who died?" Clem swallowed hard.

Ryan nodded as he began to rinse the dishes. "They were best friends. She worked on the ranch with him."

Clem realized Joanna probably had been the one who kept up the grass and flower beds and made sure the house had been painted. When she'd died, much around her had died, including her brother's soul.

"What happened?" Clem's voice was very faint, even to her ears. She wanted to know but was afraid. Awareness of his tragedies would only bind her to him in ways that she didn't want. Never in her life had she so tenaciously sought out a stranger the way she had Dexter Scott. Never in her life had she kissed a stranger, but she'd kissed Dexter Scott. And when she'd found him and kissed him, she'd known Dexter Scott wasn't a stranger at all. That was scary as hell.

"She died in a riding accident."

"I'm sorry." And Clem found that she was. She wondered what Joanna had been like. "Did she like to ride?"

"There wasn't a better rider than Joanna."

"I love to ride. I think if I were going to go, that would be the way to do it. It'd be like flying."

Ryan studied her. "You favor her a little."

Embarrassed, Clem looked away and muttered, "It's just the locket." She put her hand up to touch it, then said quietly, "He told me a little about her."

"Really?" One of Ryan's eyebrows went up. "Actually, I'm not surprised."

Clem began to understand how very private Dexter was. The fact that he'd even told her about Joanna was clearly a giant step for him, and she'd treated it as if it was normal conversation. No wonder he couldn't talk about it for more than a moment at a time.

"Why not?"

"When Dexter told us that you rode New Horse, I could tell you'd made an impression on him."

Clem furrowed her brow. "I'm not sure why that would make a difference."

Ryan looked at her in amazement. "Hell, Clem. *I* won't ride New Horse. Dexter can only ride him sometimes. The fact you rode him as if he was the tamest beast in the world blew Dex's mind. He couldn't stop talking about you after you left."

"Dexter? The same man who can barely string two sentence together?" Clem laughed.

"He talks once you get to know him."

"I didn't *know* New Horse was dangerous," Clem said. "If I had, I probably wouldn't have tried to ride him."

Ryan grinned. "Isn't that how it always is? If you'd known about Dexter before, you probably wouldn't have looked for him in the first place."

Clem stayed quiet. It wasn't true. She'd certainly been aware of his reputation but had looked for him anyway.

DEXTER LAY ON HIS BUNK and stared up at the ceiling. Once let loose, he had no way of controlling the emotions that were rolling through him. Was it bad that he'd never cried for Joanna?

The light clicked on.

"This has got to stop." Randy's voice came from the doorway.

"Go away." Dexter didn't want to be rude to his friend, but he really wasn't in the mood for Randy.

"Stop doing this to yourself. I've watched you wither away for the past three years. I think it's time for someone to tell you enough is enough."

"What the hell are you talking about?"

"I'm talking about the fact that you've withdrawn from the world so much that you can't see what a horse's behind you've become."

Dexter sat up and glared at his friend. "You act

like everything's fine, like everything's the same. Don't you even miss her?''

Dexter never saw the fist that smacked him in the mouth. ''You want to hit me back?'' Randy taunted. ''Go on. Give it your best shot.''

''Don't tempt me.'' Dexter's forearm was cocked.

''Anytime you think you can take me on, I'm ready. I'm sick and tired of walking around you. How the hell can you ask if I miss her? You don't know what I feel, because every time her name's mentioned you clam up or walk out.''

Dexter swung, but Randy ducked and caught him in a fierce bear hug. ''You know, Scott, that's the first real emotion you've shown in three years.''

''Let me go.'' Dexter jabbed his elbow into Randy's ribs. Randy didn't even flinch.

''I will when you promise you'll go invite Clem to come with us.'' The laughter in Randy's voice infuriated him.

''No.'' He flailed a little more.

Randy's bear hug tightened. ''She's not going to die the way Joanna did.''

''You know that for sure?'' Dexter felt an unbearable pressure on his chest, and it wasn't caused by Randy's massive arms. ''You can guarantee Clem won't go over a cliff the higher up we get? You saw those trails.''

"Clem's been roaming around these mountains most of her life. She can ride better than most men."

"That didn't save Joanna."

"Nothing could have saved Joanna." Randy let him go abruptly, and Dexter tumbled and fell. "Don't you know that? Nothing, not you, not me, not anybody could have saved Joanna."

Dexter lay on the ground breathing hard, trying to fight against the throbbing headache that threatened to overwhelm him.

Randy crouched next to him. "But there's time to save yourself. Joanna would have never wanted her death to affect you this way."

Dex's eyes were dry. He could feel the chill of the floor seep through to his back. "Joanna had no idea she was going to die."

"And there are worse ways to go."

"I miss her every day."

"Me, too."

Finally, Dexter struggled to sit up and Randy held out his hand. "Sorry about the fat lip," Randy apologized as he helped Dexter to his feet.

Dexter touched his mouth. It was sore. "I probably deserved it."

"Life goes on, buddy."

"I know. But I can't help thinking about Joanna."

Randy didn't say anything. He walked over to his bunk and fished around under his pillow and came up with a worn snapshot. He handed it to Dexter. "I sleep with this under my pillow every night. And every morning I say hello."

Dexter didn't want to take the picture. He hadn't seen a photograph of Joanna in three years.

"Say hello," Randy insisted, holding it out.

With the greatest reluctance, Dexter held out his hand, for the photo. He slowly brought it into his line of vision.

"There's nothing to be afraid of. She's not a ghost," Randy said.

Dexter stared at the picture and the force of Joanna's smile knocked the breath out of him.

"Beautiful, isn't she?"

Dexter nodded.

"That's what it means to be alive, Scott. It's right there in that smile."

Dexter studied the large grin, then looked at the simple round locket around her neck.

"I've still got that locket," Dexter whispered. "I take it everywhere, but I don't open it."

Randy nodded in understanding and answered Dex's original question. "Do I miss her? Hell, yes. Do I regret anything about her life? Not at all. And you should realize there's a wonderful woman out there who's full of life and can cook her ass off, but should really be riding in those mountains. If only you can put Joanna to rest.''

CLEM SAT ON THE PORCH in her mother's rocker and waited. She didn't know if Dexter would come out of the bunkhouse, but she hoped he would. Ryan had left more than an hour ago and she could hear voices and laughter drifting over from the bunkhouse. It was pretty ordinary as bunkhouses went. Ten pine bunk beds lined the large living space, and there was a big stone fireplace with a generous hearth. Clem had played there when it wasn't in use and remembered being able to stand upright in the fireplace until she was about fourteen. It was a comfortable place to hang out when it wasn't filled with the seasonal cowboys who'd come in the fall to brand and in the spring for roundup.

At those times, Clem would linger by the door listening to the men discuss loudly and colorfully their day on the range, hearing names like Beercan Ridge, Portegue Canyon and Huckabee Camp, their deep laughter surrounding her like warm smoke. Every once in a while, one of the cowboys would catch sight of her, then toss her a peppermint and tell the others to watch their language because there was a lady in the room. When their jobs were over, the cowboys and their noisy banter would be gone and it would just be her mother and father.

Now the cowboys who worked for her lived in town and drove to the ranch when they were needed. Clem rubbed her arms, starting to feel the chill of the evening. She wanted to talk to Dexter, but after glancing at her watch, she decided to give him fifteen more minutes before heading inside.

As if on cue, a solitary figure wandered out of the bunkhouse and over to the corral where New Horse was. Just from the angle of his body and his gait, Clem knew it was Dexter. She watched him pull something from his jacket pocket and hold it out to the horse. He pranced back and forth, before quickly nipping at the offering and then retreating.

It was now or never. Clem stood up and walked across the courtyard. Dexter was leaning up against the fence, elbows on the top rail, watching his horses, absently chewing on the stem of a small leaf.

Clem came up and stood next to him.

He shifted slightly to give her room, the leaf still in his mouth.

His earlier tension seemed to have subsided.

He's trying, Clem realized. *He's trying.* She could try, too. She could wait for him to heal.

As the silence lengthened, she began to think she might have to stand and wait all night.

Before she could decide what to do next, Dexter looked up at the stars. "Pretty here."

"Not like the desert," Clem conceded.

"Different, but pretty in its own right." He nodded, then shifted and glanced down at her.

With an easy hop, she climbed the fence to sit on the top rail—right in front of him where he couldn't miss her. Maybe if she stared at him long enough, he'd actually tell her why he didn't want her to go out with them.

However, once in position, Clem was unnerved. Their proximity was oddly intimate. If she put her hands out, she could wrap her arms around his neck and pull him closer until her legs straddled his waist. But she didn't. She simply hooked the heels of her boots on the next rung of the fence and used her hands to keep herself from teetering foolishly. At least this way they were almost eye to eye.

Dexter didn't move away as she'd expected. She'd thought he'd pull back and put a respectable eighteen inches between them or maybe even walk away again. Instead, he placed his hands on either side of her hips and leaned forward.

They were close. Terribly, terribly close.

Too close for anyone looking at them to believe they weren't touching. She could see the moonlight reflected in his eyes, the darkening stubble on his chin. The gentle curve of his bottom lip. What was it about that bottom lip of his? Actually it looked swollen.

She gently touched it. He winced.

"What happened?" she asked.

"A gift from Randy," he said with a real smile.

She frowned. "I hope you hit him back."

Dexter laughed. "I tried. He's big but he's quick."

"I hope you deserved it, then."

"He thought I did."

They lapsed into silence.

"Are we alone?" he asked finally, his voice low and husky.

Mint.

Dexter Scott was chewing on a spring of peppermint, which grew in abundance around the property. She fought the urge to kiss him. "I think so. Everyone's fat and happy after that supper."

She could feel his breath on her cheek.

"That meal was good. Best I've had in a while."

"I haven't had anyone to cook for in ages. Ryan made quick work of the dishes and the mess."

As they talked of inconsequential things, a new tension developed between them. One that wasn't based on their differing opinions. Clem wasn't sure her heart could take it.

"Well, I guess I better turn in, too," Dexter said, and pushed himself away from her. The chill of the night air hit her right in the face.

"Morning comes early," he continued. He

shoved his hands into his pockets and rocked back on his heels to study the stars. ‘‘We have a lot of work to do, so we need to get an early start in the morning.’’

‘‘I’m an early riser,’’ Clem said.

Dexter regarded her. ‘‘And you’re telling me this because?’’

‘‘I’m going, too.’’ She made her voice soft but determined.

‘‘Can I offer you a piece of advice?’’ he asked in a voice so strained that she felt it rumble through her very soul.

‘‘What?’’

‘‘Persuasion is always more effective than force.’’

Clem flushed. ‘‘What are you saying?’’

‘‘I’m saying that for someone who wants something real bad, you sure aren’t going about asking for it very nicely.’’

CHAPTER SEVEN

WHILE SHE CONSIDERED his comment, Dexter's face remained impassive, as if emotions were simply not allowed to pass across it. She swallowed hard and then bestowed on him a wry smile.

"Excuse me," she said, lowering her voice. "And do you have any suggestions on how I might ask you more nicely? What if I said please?"

He moved closer to her but still didn't touch her, though that hardly seemed possible. "I'm not sure that a simple please will do it."

"Not even if I said it really nicely?" Clem shifted. His scrutiny was disconcerting, and Clem felt the force of his presence surround her, engulf her. It was almost as if she could feel him touch her cheek, her temples, the nape of her neck. But his hands remained in his pockets. Then his gaze went to her locket.

She self-consciously brought a hand up to it. "My parents gave this to me," she said in explanation.

He didn't say anything.

She cleared her throat. "You probably believe I

won't be very good. But I will be. I'm very familiar with the area, no matter what you think about me." She couldn't help the defensiveness that crept into her voice.

"You have no idea what I think about you."

"I've got a pretty good idea."

"Really, now?"

She swallowed, trying to moisten her throat. "I bet you think I'm some sort of princess who's been waited on all her life. And you think I'm only happy if the world revolves around me. Mostly, you think I shouldn't be doing this job."

"And you'd be wrong on all accounts."

TIME SEEMED TO STOP as she lifted her eyes to his. If she hadn't had ligament and tissue holding her bones together, what she saw in his eyes would have made her melt. She could see life and love dancing there, but she also saw fear. She swallowed hard, trying not to look away from the intensity in his stare.

"Clem." His voice was so low she could barely hear it.

"Yes?"

"We ride at five." With that he pushed himself away from her, and strode toward the bunkhouse.

THERE WAS PANDEMONIUM in the courtyard the next morning as Randy and Ryan hitched the trailers to the truck and, loaded up the horses. For two men, they made a lot of noise. Clem enjoyed every sound. When Dexter walked into her line of sight, she tried to ignore the alarm bells that went off. By the grim set of Dexter's mouth, Clem knew that this morning was all about business. He was here to find the cows.

The sound of the horse's hooves on the trailer ramps brought back fond memories to Clem. When she was young, she had loved to be around cowboys. She loved how they talked to one another and to their horses. How they smelled, and how they teased her.

Odd she would marry a man who wore Italian silk rather than cotton and leather, a man who could never quite capture the right rhythm to make profanity sound like music. Looking back, she realized Nick and his friends weren't men—not real men, anyway. She'd been so anxious to get away from home and prove herself different, she'd turned her back on her true self, making her easy prey for someone like Nick. Now she understood what her father had meant when he'd said his son-in-law had never felt "right" to him.

She was certain her father would find everything about Dexter Scott and the Miller brothers "right." They were an impressive sampling of the male species, all towering height, broad shoulders and muscled arms that easily took the weight of whatever load needed to be hauled. So fit they could keep up their continuous banter in spite of the heavy work.

"Clem, shake a leg," Randy hollered at her. "You're riding shotgun with Dex."

Shotgun with Dexter. Clem raised a hand in acknowledgement, then walked over to Dexter's truck.

"Get on in," Dexter invited.

She'd been in his truck before and was prepared for the worst. To her amazement, he'd thoroughly cleaned the interior. No leftover fast-food wrappers, no soda cans, no layer of dust thick enough to write in. In fact, it seemed as if he'd shined the seats, because she kept sliding forward.

"Like what you've done with your truck," she commented when he climbed in next to her.

He shifted into a lower gear to compensate for the load that they were hauling. He gave her a small grin. "Guess I didn't notice the dust until you did."

"It's your truck." She gave a shrug and ignored the small drizzle of pleasure she received from the thought he'd cleaned it up for her.

"But you're riding in it."

Clem smiled but didn't say anything, content to let Dexter focus on his driving.

After a few minutes, Dexter asked, "Where to?"

"We'll go about three miles down this road, then cut left at a service road. That will take us up about halfway up the mountain and drop us right about where you spotted evidence of the herd yesterday."

Dexter nodded, and they drove the rest of the way in silence.

Clem was getting used to the quiet. Nick had been a talker. He'd woken up talking, gone to sleep talking. She'd come to believe that he allocated himself a certain number of words to use in a day—and he couldn't sleep until he met his quota. Amazing how she could feel so lonely when he was talking at her all the time. She didn't feel lonely now, and Dexter hadn't said more than ten words to her.

She shifted in her seat.

"You okay?" Dexter sent her a quick glance before he turned his attention avoiding a pothole.

She nodded. "Fine, just fine."

And that was the truth.

When they reached the plateau and began to saddle up, Clem pointed north and said, "We should go up there. You'll be able to get a bird's-eye view of the whole valley."

Randy nodded. Mounting Shuckabur, he waited for Clem to lead the way. If she had felt any trepidation about guiding them, it evaporated once she was on Archie. She'd spent her whole childhood wandering through these mountains. And even though it'd been a few years since she'd been this high up, the familiarity of the terrain was very comforting to her. She inhaled deeply. Even though they were only a thousand feet up the air smelled different.

"It's gorgeous," Dexter said next to her. His eyes on her face.

She smiled. "I can't believe that I've been away for so long."

"But now you're back."

"Yes. Now I'm back."

By the third cowless hour, their good spirits had started to wear a little thin.

"I think we need to go in another direction," Ryan said after he dismounted to study some tracks. "There's nothing around except deer."

"I wouldn't expect the cows to come up this high," Randy added.

Clem felt awful. It had been her suggestion that had brought them here, which was quite a distance from their original position. "We can go down this way and get close to where we were about an hour ago, but it's a little steep."

"What's a little steep?" Dexter asked.

She led them to the path and pointed down. It was the equivalent to a dead man's run at a ski resort. If a horse stumbled, there'd be nothing to break the fall except for the odd boulder and some wild sage. The one time she'd taken it she'd barely survived.

Randy whistled, then flashed an I-dare-you smile at Ryan. "That little slope? Why, that's nothing but a hill. Last one to the bottom is a rotten egg." Without giving himself a moment to change his mind, he spurred Shuckabur and was gone. Ryan followed, shouting good-natured obscenities at Randy the whole way down.

"Go next," Dexter instructed.

Clementine hesitated. It wasn't just a little steeper than she'd remembered, it was a *lot* steeper. She'd been a teenager when she'd tried it, and not nearly as concerned with her mortality as she was now.

She flashed Dexter a fake smile and countered, "You go. I'll be right behind you."

DEXTER REGARDED CLEMENTINE. He'd been around enough frightened animals to know she was terrified.

"Don't look," he advised. "Trust Archie to know what to do."

"I'm not scared," she denied. "I just don't want to go first. You go on. I'll be right behind you."

Dexter didn't believe her cheerful tone for a second. "No. I want you to go."

Clem was silent for a long time, her eyes fixed

on the path. She bit her lip and then looked at him helplessly. "I can't."

"Why not?"

"I lied before. I'm scared."

Dexter chuckled.

"It's okay to be scared," he said. "Just don't let it keep you from doing what you need to be doing." He stopped, struck by the words. Once, long ago, he'd said as much to Joanna. He frowned, trying to push away another memory.

"I'm not going that way, Dex. I'm not." Joanna's lip trembled. She looked very small on the saddle.

He felt awful. Joanna was only eleven, too young to go on the trip, but they were here now and there was no other way home.

"You need to be brave," he said. "I know you can do this."

"I don't want to." Joanna started to cry.

"No, no crying." He couldn't believe he'd made her cry. "Just suck it up and do it." He knew he sounded harsh, but it was the only way to get her down this mountain—the only way to make her independent.

Tears pouring down her face, she took the plunge. Halfway down, he heard her scream with delight.

When he met her at the bottom, the tears had dried up.

"Can I do that again, Dex? Can I do it again?"

"Hey! Where are you guys?" Randy yelled up the embankment. "Ryan's found something."

"Come on."

"No." Clem sat frozen, clutching the horn of her saddle. "You go. I'll meet you back at the truck in an hour or so."

"Nope." Dexter grinned. Then he hooked one of her reins and uttered a short command to Archie. "We're going down." And together they went over the side of the mountain.

CLEM'S STOMACH FLEW to her throat as Archie headed straight down. She felt like she was on a roller coaster but wasn't strapped in. She choked back a scream and hung on for dear life, feeling Archie scramble for his footing. Halfway down, Dexter flipped her the reins, and although she grabbed them, she just closed her eyes and let Archie do the work. She braced herself for the inevitable fall, but it never happened.

At the bottom, Dexter turned and said with a laugh. "Now, that wasn't so bad, was it?"

If Clem had been able to form words, she would have disagreed.

"Breathe," he reminded her. "You won't feel so sick."

She inhaled sharply, amazed he could tell she was nauseous.

Randy rode up to them. "This way. Ryan's found something."

"Go ahead," she gasped. "I'm right behind you."

With a nod, Dexter followed Randy.

A few moments later, Clem and Archie trotted over to the men, and she finally realized she was out of her league. These guys *were* elite cowboys, able to do anything and everything on horseback. She'd always thought Archie was fit and well-trained, but he was hard-pressed to keep up with the other horses.

"What did you find?" she asked, grateful her breath was under control.

"They're really close," Ryan said. "It seems as if the cattle cut through here. What's that way?"

"It's an old box canyon. There's a really narrow fissure that I was able to squeeze through when I was younger. But the only other way in is through the creek bed."

"Let's go."

They rode for another half hour before they ended up on the creek bank across from the entrance to the canyon.

"There can't be any feed around here," Randy said, looking around.

"Much of this is volcanic rock," Clem said. She directed Archie to walk into the shallow creek. "One thing the area does have is plenty of water."

"Where are we in relation to the house?" Ryan asked.

"About twenty miles as the crow flies, but we're actually not that far from the trucks."

"Really? How's the path from there to here."

"Well, you just rode part of it," Clem said.

"So that plateau would be as good a place as any to set up the corral."

"We could even bring a truck most of the way," Randy suggested.

Dexter frowned. "Maybe Clem's truck. It's pretty narrow. But the full-size trucks would never make it. The last thing we need is a truck on its head."

"Let's find the cows first. They've got to be close." Ryan sniffed the air. "I can smell them. What'll we find if we follow the creek?"

Clem thought and then smiled. "I don't know how I forgot, but there's a small pasture that dries up in the heat of the summer. I bet the rain we had has rejuvenated the grass."

"There's the feed." Ryan nodded.

"Water, food. That's all they need," Randy spurred Shuckabur forward. "Let's go get them. Clem, lead the way."

Clem was more than happy to oblige. At least this was something she could do. She took them down the creek to a small valley. When they got there, she almost cried with relief.

Hundreds of fat, healthy cows, all with her family's brand, grazed. They looked up at the new activity, but then dismissed the newcomers as no threat and went back to chewing.

"We found your cows," Randy said.

"Isn't that a beautiful sight?" she asked. If they got these cows in quickly, she just might be able to put out another herd before her parents came to town. Her elation bubbled up and she laughed. "Ryan, you are a wonder. How many do you think there are?"

Ryan had been estimating apparently. "Near four hundred. That means there's another pocket of them still hiding."

"Thank you, thank you, thank you. If you were closer, I'd kiss you!" Clem actually clapped her hands in excitement.

"No kissing or clapping yet." Dexter moved Calisto right next to Archie. "Finding them was the easy part. Now we're going to have to get them back home."

"That's your job, Dex. I've done mine," Ryan smiled with mock smugness.

They spent the next three hours scouting the area.

After Dexter called a break, they chewed on venison jerky, and began to plan, Clem just listening as they batted around ideas. Finally a real strategy began to emerge.

Dexter looked up to the sun. "We should head back. There's only a couple more hours of daylight, and I don't want to be stuck in these canyons after dark. Plus, Clem has to get on the phone. We need those men for tomorrow."

THE NEXT DAY, five men joined the team, and the morning was spent setting up the pens on the plateau they'd parked on the day before.

"So what's the plan?" Ryan asked Dexter.

"We'll have to try to get them to follow the creek," Dexter said. "We need to put three riders on each side. Randy, Ryan and I'll be in the back and then we'll let the dogs go. They'll do the majority of the job. If everything goes as planned, we can get them on the path right to the pens."

Clem nodded, more excited than she'd been in a long time. She understood Dex's plan and she knew it was going to work.

"The riders on the left will have to be very careful to block the entrance to the canyon. These cows might stampede, and we don't want them to head in there. It would be a big, fat waste of time waiting for them to find their way out."

"I think we should start with just a few and then go back for more," Ryan said.

Randy disagreed. "I think once the dogs start in, it's going to be all or nothing."

"But we don't know if we can control the flow." Ryan was ever the conservative.

"We'll soon see. Once the dogs get going we'll just have to try to keep the cows going in the right direction." Randy's attitude was practical.

Dexter turned to Clem. "They're your cows. What do you think? Small groups or the whole shebang?"

She shook her head. "I leave it up to you."

"Make a decision," he said, his voice mild but insistent.

"I agree with Randy," she said slowly. "I think once the dogs start barking, all the cows will make a break for it. We won't have a choice to take them out in controlled numbers."

Dexter nodded. "Okay. We try for the whole herd. Probably the worst that can happen is we'll lose a few."

Clem's heart was thumping hard as she positioned herself next to two hands.

At Dexter's signal, the dogs raced forward.

The commotion was unreal, but the cows did begin to bunch together. One cow tried to escape, but Clem was able to cut off its path. When it rejoined the group, Clem felt a thrill she hadn't known before.

She was so busy watching her part of the line that she wasn't aware of what was going on elsewhere, but she began to worry when she realized she couldn't hear the cows enter the creek. The water level was low, but she should have been able to hear splashing.

The yelp of a dog had her peering through the dust, but she couldn't see anything. She had to abandon her search, though, when a bunch of cows began to break left.

''*No!*'' she shouted. The creek was straight ahead. She needed to keep them heading for the creek. But all her efforts were futile, and she watched with increasing dismay as they funneled through the small opening to the box canyon, where there was nothing but sandstone and space.

Ryan reined his horse right next to her, his eyes watching, evaluating. ''I knew he was wrong,'' he said, his voice irritated.

Clem looked around her, trying to find Dexter's familiar gray hat. ''Where's Dexter?'' she asked Ryan. ''Where's Randy?''

Ryan grinned at her. ''They're trying to turn the cows from the other side. I think they figured they could block the escape route and get the cows to head back this way.''

"It won't work," Clem protested. "Dex and Randy'll be crushed."

"Why? There should be room for all of them." He made a small attempt at a joke. "I know Randy's been eating a lot lately—"

"You don't understand," Clem swallowed, trying to control her panic. "It looks big, but the further in you go, the narrower it gets. There'll be nowhere for the guys to go."

"We need to see if we can at least turn the cows that haven't made it through," Ryan said, spurring his horses. "You go from the south."

He quickly explained the plan to the other men, then waited for everyone to get into place. "Now!"

Without another thought, she rode Archie directly at the cows that were still heading toward the canyon. Her effort was rewarded when a cow veered off in the other direction. That got the rest of them running away from the canyon entrance.

"Is there another way into the canyon?" Ryan shouted, after they'd managed to turn the remaining cows. "We need to get to Randy and Dex."

Clem didn't answer. The first time she'd been in the canyon the creek had been high. The only way in had been a fissure just big enough for a man walking a horse to get through.

"It's got to be here," she muttered, searching desperately. "I know it's here somewhere. It's around a rock. A large boulder.'' She drew in a deep breath. Sandstone boulders eroded with time, and she hadn't thought about this entrance in almost fifteen years.

Then she saw a round sandstone rock, hidden beneath the bushes. Scrambling off Archie, she hoped it was what she was looking for. Ryan dismounted and joined her.

''What are we looking for?'' he asked.

''A fissure.'' She fought her way past the brush, ignoring the burs and branches, until she got the boulder.

''It's a big fissure, another entrance to the canyon. But it might have closed, eroded. Oh, let it be here. Please let it—here it is!''

She pulled away thorny vines that had got hold of the sandstone, obscuring the opening. She grabbed her hunting knife from her saddle and began slashing away at the vines. What she found wasn't encouraging. The opening was smaller than she'd thought. She held her breath and started to squeeze through.

A hand yanked her back.

''What?'' she demanded.

''That looks unsafe,'' Ryan said. He had a small shovel. ''Let me go first.''

Systematically he began to whack at the walls.

The sandstone rained down on top of him. "This could collapse."

"We only need it to hold until we can get them out."

"It's going to be a tight squeeze for the horses."

"I don't care about the horses!" Clem yelled, pushing past him.

The fissure was dark and narrow, and condensation dripped on her head. Apparently this was the perfect condition for the vines. She began hacking at them, fear of what she was going to find adding strength to her frenzied strokes. What seemed like hours later, she emerged to see that Dexter and Randy had only a limited amount of room to maneuver. Despite the hands' best efforts, some cows were still trying to crowd into the canyon.

"Dexter! Randy!" she hollered, desperate to get their attention. Belatedly she realized that theirs wasn't the only attention that she caught. A cow had its eyes trained on her.

DEXTER WASN'T SURE how Clem had managed to get into the canyon. She was right in the path of a cow who had nowhere to go but *through* her. Using every skill he possessed, he managed to bump and jostle his way through the cows to get to Clem. At the last possible moment, he threw his rope and managed to snap the horn of the charging cow.

"Get the hell out of there!" he yelled.

Clem nodded and signaled for him to follow her. She disappeared into the vines.

Then Randy shouted, "She's found a way out."

Dexter let go of the rope and followed Randy, sliding off Calisto right before the opening.

Clem met them, holding the vines aside.

"You have to lead Calisto and Shuckabur through," she said. "It's really narrow."

"Narrow is better than dead," Randy commented. "I can feel cow breath on my neck. Scoot on through, Clem. You are a lifesaver."

The horses shot out of the small crevice like a cork out of a champagne bottle. They shook their manes to rid themselves of the debris, all the time whinnying their intense displeasure. Ryan grabbed their reins, calming them with a soothing voice.

Dexter and Randy collapsed on the ground, looking up at the sky.

Ryan stared down at them and addressed his brother, "You never listen to me do you?"

"It wasn't so bad," Randy said confidently. "I knew there had to be a way out."

"You did not," Dexter accused with a grin. But the grin faded when he caught sight of Clem. She looked like she was going to pass out. Her face was ashen gray.

He stared at her, thinking she was the most beautiful woman in the world. ''Are you okay?'' His voice was gruff.

She nodded, but he didn't believe her. Finally some color came back into her cheeks.

''That was quick thinking on your part, Clem,'' Randy complimented her. ''I think we owe you our lives.''

''I *know* you owe me your lives,'' Clem said. She plopped down next to them. ''This isn't worth it, guys. No herd is.''

Dexter could feel her tremble next to him. He grabbed her hand, surprised at how cold it was.

''It's part of the thrill,'' he said gently. ''We're fine.''

Tears welled up in her eyes. She shook her head. ''This isn't thrilling. This is scary. If Ryan hadn't been able to turn away so much of the herd, you both would have been trapped or killed. This is too dangerous. I think we should just shoot them. I'll take my losses.''

''No!'' all three men said in unison.

''We've come this far. We'll get them out of the canyon.'' Ryan nodded.

''What are you going to do? Bribe them?'' Clem's voice was high, the pitch alone evidence of her shock.

Dexter shook his head. ''Won't need to. They're not happy where they are, so they'll eventually find their way out. It's easy. We just have to wait. And then we'll take them twenty or thirty at a time, the way we originally planned."

"Twenty trips rather than one?" Clem asked.

"We have the time," Ryan said gently. "And you'll have your herd."

When Clem didn't respond, Dexter patted her hand. "Please, Clem. It's going to be smooth sailing from here. You've had a bad scare. But this is just part of the job."

Finally, she swallowed and stood up, dusting herself off. "Well, then," she said. "I guess we'd better go back and see what we can do about the others."

THE REST OF THE MORNING went slowly. The cows that hadn't gone into the canyon had scattered into the mountains. That was just as well for Clem. She still couldn't shake the stark fear that had overtaken her when she'd realized Dexter and Randy were trapped. The men seemed to know this and each spent a few moments reassuring her. By the time the first cows began to venture out of the canyon, Clem had recovered her sense of self. Working together they managed to herd together the cows. Then Dexter and Randy, with the help of three dogs, took them down the path to the waiting corral.

They came back nodding. ''It worked. We've got ten down.''

While they'd been gone, Clem, Randy and the hands had managed to gather up another ten.

And so back and forth they worked, until they'd rounded up fifty and daylight had started to fade.

''We better call it quits,'' Randy said. ''It gets dark pretty darn quick up here.''

''Maybe a couple of us should stay out and watch these,'' one of the hired hands suggested.

Ryan shook his head. ''I don't think it's necessary. They're not going anywhere and if they decide to, two guys aren't going to stop them. We've put in a good day's work. Let's go on home.''

Clem was exhausted once they got back to the trailers. She didn't think she even had the strength to lift the saddle off Archie. She leaned her head against it. Maybe if she rested first.

''Are you trying to levitate it using just your brain?'' Randy asked, as he gently brushed her aside and removed the saddle.

She smiled at him. ''I am so glad you guys made it out.''

''Thanks to you. Ryan tells me it was all your doing.''

She shook her head. ''I think it was Archie. I was frightened out of my mind.'' Archie nickered at the sound of his name. She patted him on the nose as she led him into the trailer. "You get an extra brushing and an extra bucket of oats tonight."

Dexter waited until she got out of the trailer. Then he closed the door with a definitive slam. He walked next to her, opening up the passenger side of the truck. With an easy heft, he deposited her on the seat.

She smiled wryly. "I'm exhausted."

"You worked hard," he said as he started the truck. He stared in his side-view mirror, studying the fifty head in the corral. "They are beauties."

Clem had already closed her eyes. She was sick to death of those cows.

"We're going to have to figure out how to get them from the plateau to your pasture," Dexter said as he pulled out.

"Can't we just send them down the road?" Clem yawned.

He nodded. "In tens and twenties again. It's going to be slow. Maybe we can have several groups go one after another."

"Sounds like a plan. I can't wait to get rid of them."

There was a long silence. Dexter cleared his throat and said gruffly, "You did good out there."

She smiled at him. "Thanks."

"You look like you were born for the work. How come you've never done it before?"

She made a face and rested back against his slippery seat. ''During college, I was dazzled by an intellectual business major. After that, I only came back here for holidays.''

''You're easily dazzled?''

She nodded. ''At eighteen, I was. Nick, was, is a very charming man, quite a talker, and I'd grown up around cowboys. My dad had warned me about the cowboys, but not about the slick city boys.'' She gave him a small smile. ''I was a farm girl, and I had a really hard time adjusting, until Nick picked me out of all the other freshmen girls. The rest is history.''

''History?''

''I quit school to get married and we got really rich in San Jose on the dot.com wave. Then he fell in love with one of his colleagues and he left me. Twelve years gone—poof!''

''He must be a fool.''

She shook her head. ''No. He's just a man who can talk well.''

She reflected on what that meant. Nick was *just* a man who could talk well. He could talk himself into and out of everything. Funny, how she'd always thought that if the people around her talked more, she'd feel less isolated, less lonely. Yet here she sat next to a man whose silence filled her with a complete sense of herself.

CHAPTER EIGHT

CLEM STEPPED OUT of the shower and felt like a new woman. She could almost forget this morning's terrifying incident. Almost. She hurt all over. Her back, her shoulder, her neck. She'd found muscles she didn't even realize she had.

He must be a fool.

Clem smiled and fastened her locket around her neck. In his silent way, Dexter was reaching out to her. Maybe, just maybe, he liked her. With a light heart, she walked down the stairs, wondering what in the world they would eat for dinner. She'd told Dex to give her an hour, but the shower had taken up twenty precious minutes.

She had some steaks defrosting in the refrigerator along with some more green beans and a couple of sweet potatoes. She could do something with that. As she got closer to the kitchen, the aroma of sizzling steaks assaulted her. She pushed open the door and found Randy and Ryan. Both had cleaned up, their hair slicked back from a shower, their clothes rumpled but clean.

"What are you guys doing?"

Ryan looked at Randy, whose grin was a mile wide.

"It was a surprise. Steak and eggs. Ryan's making sweet potato fries. Hope you don't mind."

"Don't mind?" Clem laughed. "Do you see this smile? It's a relief. I was just wondering what to make you."

"You don't have to do the cooking. We're perfectly capable."

Clem perched on a chair. "I can see that. Where did you pick up your culinary skills?"

There was a protracted silence as the brothers exchanged a look. Both of their faces reddened. "You answer that," Randy said, passing the question to Ryan.

"The cook," Ryan supplied with a grin.

"The cook?"

Both brothers looked sheepish. "Our family has a little money."

"A little money?" Clem considered them.

"Okay. A lot of money. Bakersfield oil, mainly."

"And you do this because..."

"Well, we've got to eat sometime," Randy said, deliberately misunderstanding her.

"You know what I mean. You rope wild cows because..."

They were silent.

Finally, Ryan said, his voice light, "We like it."

"We had, shall we say, a, um, turbulent adolescence." Randy flipped a steak.

"And our parents shipped us to one of those cowboy boot camps to straighten us out. We liked it."

"And the rest is history," Randy finished, cracking an egg with one hand.

"I could eat a horse," Dexter announced as he walked in the back door.

Clem couldn't help but give him a wide smile. He, too, had cleaned up. And he'd taken the time to shave.

"A cow will have to do," Randy said. He handed Dexter a plate of steaks. "Take that into the dining room. And no, it's not all for you. Clem gets first shot at the steaks, since it's thanks to her that we're here to enjoy them."

Clem hopped off the stool and started to rummage through the drawers for forks and knives. She grabbed the napkins out of another drawer and headed into the dining room. Once she got there, Dexter took everything from her and proceeded to set the table.

Suddenly, as they both realized they were alone, an awkward silence descended.

"You clean up real nice," Clem said. Her voice sounded loud.

Dexter glanced up. "Thanks," he replied.

A long moment later, he added, "You do, too."

"Thanks."

Nothing else to say, he paid particular attention to aligning the forks and knives vertically.

They both looked up when Randy burst into the room, carrying a plate of eggs in one hand and some sweet potato fries in the other. Ryan followed with the familiar maps.

"It's a working dinner, as usual," Ryan said as they were all seated.

The maps were laid out, the canyon marked, along with the count. Clem listened to the rumble of their voices, a wave of good feeling trickling through her. She rested her head on her hand as she listened.

"Go to bed, Clem." Dexter's voice caused her eyes to snap open.

"What?"

"Go to bed. We're going to have a really early start in the morning."

She stood up, looking at her plate. She'd hardly eaten anything, but right now the urge to sleep was stronger than her stomach's growling. "I guess I'm a little more tired than I thought I'd be." She picked up her plate, but Dexter took it from her.

"We'll get the dishes. You just get some sleep."

With a sleepy wave, she obeyed, climbing the stairs with heavy legs. It seemed to take all the effort in the world to undress, but Clem went through the motions, finally pulling on her flannel pajamas before flopping into the bed.

RANDY ELBOWED DEXTER. "You should go see if she makes it to her room."

Dexter scowled at Randy.

Randy raised his eyebrow. "I'm serious. You should go see. It wouldn't hurt if you went to tuck her in."

Dexter ignored him and took her plate and his own to the kitchen. Since she'd hardly taken two bites, he covered it in plastic wrap and popped it in the refrigerator. She'd probably be hungry later on.

Twenty minutes later, the kitchen was clean, and they all quietly left through the back door.

"Dexter, I think you should start us a fire," Randy said when they got back to the bunkhouse. "And Ryan, I think you should find your guitar."

"And what will you be doing?"

"Just drawing." Randy grinned. He rifled through one of his bags and pulled out a sketchbook and some pencils.

So Dexter started a fire, Ryan played his guitar and Randy sketched the scene. A couple of hours later when the fire began to die down, Dexter scooted to the fireplace to put a new log on the embers.

"Hold that right there," Randy commanded. His head tilted.

"What?"

"Hold it. That's a terrific pose."

"It's not a pose."

"The firelight is doing awesome things to your arm and face."

"It's also hot." Dexter couldn't be annoyed with Randy. He was used to it. Then he asked facetiously, "Do you want me to put my hat on, too?"

Randy nodded. "That'd be a great touch."

Ryan leaned back, grabbed Dex's hat and plopped it on his head.

Randy grinned. "It's crooked."

Ryan straightened it out, pushing it down on Dex's forehead.

"No. I like it better up, so you can see his face."

"Can I put my arm down now?" Dexter asked as Ryan shifted the hat again. His shoulder was starting to ache as he kept the log extended.

"Just a minute," Randy said, his eyes moving from Dexter's form to his pad. "It's all in the name of art."

"I'm going to drop this log in the fire," Dexter threatened. "Any second now."

"One more minute."

"I don't have another minute in me." His arm

was starting to tremble and his legs were about to give out.

"What are you guys doing?" a soft voice asked behind him.

As he'd predicted, Dexter's legs gave out. He dropped the log and ended up on the ground.

CLEM STOOD UNCERTAINLY at the door, a coat over her pajamas, her feet stuck into ankle-high sheepskin slippers, holding the plate of dinner she'd warmed in the microwave and a glass of milk. She'd woken up starving and had gone to fix herself a sandwich only to find her plate. Then she'd sat at the dining room table to eat and heard the music from the bunkhouse.

Two bites later, she could stand it no longer. She pulled on her coat and headed for the bunkhouse.

The door was closed, but she could see the fire going and she heard the laughter as the men talked. She almost turned around, but then decided she'd much rather be inside with them than eating by herself in that big, empty house.

"I guess you can say you've actually managed to knock Dexter Scott on his butt," Randy chortled.

Dexter, his face beet red, scrambled to his feet, jamming the hat down further on his head, and sat on a stool next to the fire. He wouldn't look at her, overly absorbed in adjusting the logs on the fire.

"Come on in," Ryan invited. He placed a small table in front of a bunk and patted the bed. "Sit down and enjoy your meal."

"I'm not intruding?" she asked as she did as he'd indicated.

"Not at all. We're just talking and singing."

"Don't stop on my account," Clem said, and sat there appreciating the peace that seemed to flourish in their presence. She took a bite of steak. Ryan struck a few chords and Randy flipped to another sheet and started to draw.

She chewed in silence, watching Dexter watch the fire.

"It's good steak," she commented. "I like the seasonings you used."

"Thanks," Randy said, still sketching. He had a pencil in his mouth, and he was squinting at the paper.

Except for the plucking of the guitar, no one said anything.

Clem finished her plate and sat further back on the bunk so she could prop her back against the wall. A yawn overtook her. She should go back. She should just get up and go back, but the music was lovely and the bunkhouse warm.

Even the lumpy cot felt like heaven.

"Hey, Clem!"

Her eyes opened up and she yawned again. She looked in the direction of the voice.

Randy was standing over her. "Why don't you lie down? Put your head that way." He moved the pillow from the head of the bed to the foot. He plumped it up.

It was too inviting to refuse. Her head felt like it weighed a hundred pounds. She sighed with contentment. Able to keep only one eye open, she looked at Randy, who had changed angles and was obviously drawing her.

"What'cha doin'?" she mumbled.

"You're a great model. I don't think you're going to move from that pose," Randy said.

"I'm suppos' to just stay?"

"Yep."

"Oh." She yawned again and found her eye closing.

TWENTY MINUTES LATER Randy was done.

"Now what are you going to do with her?" Dexter whispered. "She's on my bed."

Randy grinned at him. "She's a great subject, don't you think?" He showed Dexter the page containing several sketches of Clem.

Dexter studied them, then looked at the bottom where Randy had signed and titled the set. *Sleeping Beauty.*

Dexter had always known that his friend was talented, but he was amazed that Randy had managed to capture Clementine's soft vulnerability.

"For you," Randy said, his voice gruff as he tore the page out of the sketchbook.

Dexter accepted the drawing, his throat working as he held back his emotions.

Randy hit him in the arm. "I know, man, I know."

All three men looked down at Clementine.

"So do we wake her up?" Dexter asked Ryan.

Ryan just smiled and plucked at a few more notes. "If I was you and I'm not, but if I was, I'd just take her up to her room."

Dexter looked at them, appalled. "As in carry her?"

"She could hardly weigh more than a smidgen, wouldn't you say, Ryan?"

Ryan shrugged. "Maybe a smidgen and a half."

Randy leaned over her. "If you don't want to carry her, Scott, I'm up to the task."

Dexter elbowed Randy out of the way.

"You're not touching her." He kneeled beside her and shook her shoulder. "Clem?"

"She's out."

"You could always just sleep on the top bunk," Randy said. "Then she could wake up here.

Though, I think she'd be *much* more comfortable in her own bed. Don't you think so, Ryan?''

Dexter scowled at them as he slid his arms under her legs and her back and hefted her up.

She weighed more than a smidgen, but not much more than a sack of grain. Randy opened the door for him and whispered in his ear, ''We've got you on the clock, man.''

If Dexter could have, he would have given him an obscene gesture.

He walked as quickly as he could, into the house, up the stairs and then stopped in the dark hall. He'd never been to the second story. He peeked into one bedroom after another. When he saw one with a rumpled bed, he took her in and gently laid her down. He puffed from the exertion and looked around. She had a wonderful view of the courtyard.

He studied the pictures on her dresser. There was a picture of her and Archie, when Archie was just a colt. Clem's face was all smiles. She loved that horse, and Dexter admired her for the depth of that love. Then he went back to the bed. She was dead asleep, but hardly looked comfortable with her coat bunched up under her.

He pulled off her slippers and then eased off her jacket, rolling her one way first and the other way. She didn't wake. Her pajama top lifted up, exposing the smooth curve of her stomach, the dimple of her navel. He was mesmerized by that navel. He wanted to run his finger around it, but contented himself with pulling down her pajama top.

Funny, she worked so hard, so effortlessly yet he still often thought of her as frail. He wondered why. Looking at her now, Dex saw that work had taken its toll on her. Clem's face was thin, accentuated by dark circles under her eyes that wouldn't be erased by one night's sleep. "Under the covers you go, Sleeping Beauty," he whispered as he moved her legs.

She purred with contentment as he pulled the covers over her shoulders.

It wasn't proper to tuck someone in without a kiss, right? He pushed her hair out of her eyes. He was aiming for her forehead, but somehow he caught her on the mouth. Just a touch of his lips to hers. That's all. Nothing more to it.

But as he straightened, he saw her eyes were open.

"Hi," she breathed, blinking.

"Hi." He backed away, like a cat burglar caught in the act. "Good night, Clem." He turned and walked out of the room as quickly as he could.

THE NEXT MORNING, Dexter was all business, and Clem didn't have time to be disappointed because once they got to the plateau Dexter split them up into sets of threes, one group to bring the cattle down the creek to the plateau and the other to take the cattle from the plateau to the ranch pasture. However, she couldn't stop the pleasure that spread through her when she thought of Dexter's stolen kiss.

"We're two men short today, so everyone's got to do their jobs," Dexter directed. "Randy, take Willie and Joe. Ryan and I'll take Clem to get the cattle."

At least she'd ended up on his team.

Forty minutes later, they rode past the canyon, and Clem was relieved to find that most of the cows had come back to the little knoll. Ryan checked in the canyon, but no cows had stayed in there.

The cows seemed to remember what had happened the last time humans had entered the knoll, because they started to scatter. A group of twenty bolted toward the mountains, but the dogs went to work, cutting them off and leaving the creek as the only other avenue of escape. Clem was posted in front of the canyon opening and—with a lot of help from Archie—managed to keep the cows from veering inside. With growing admiration, Clem watched Dexter and Ryan handle the cows, working in tandem as if they were linked telepathically.

"Come on, Clem, get the tail end," Dexter called to her, and she and Archie moved into position. Together they forced the stragglers to catch up with the little herd.

As the day wore on, it became apparent the new plan was a success. But it was slow work on both ends. Randy and the hands were having just as difficult a time getting their groups from the pasture to the ranch.

"It's like they don't have an ounce of herding instinct among them," Randy said, frustrated. "They all just want to go in their own direction. Even the dogs are beat."

The dogs did look worn-out. Every chance they got, they headed for the shade to rest.

"We better call it a day," Ryan said. "The horses are tired, too."

"But we've only moved about forty cows," Dexter said.

Randy shook his head. "I don't want to risk the dogs. They're the only things keeping the cows in line. We need more men."

"I can call this afternoon and see if I can round up some more," Clem volunteered.

Ryan looked at Dexter. "That might be for the best."

Dexter looked up at the sun. "I hate to lose that much daylight and it feels like it's going to rain."

"That would be bad," Randy commented.

If they were having this much trouble getting the

cows through the creek bed when it was just a trickle, how hard was it going to be when the water was waist deep?

The atmosphere was somber when they packed it up for the day. As soon as they got back, Clem got on the phone, following up old leads, looking for extra men. By dinnertime, she'd thought she found six more. However, despite the extra men, the next few days were filled with more disappointments than successes. The cows had taken to hiding, so the cowboys actually had to wrangle them out one by one. The plan of moving them in groups of twenty dwindled to groups of ten, then dropped to five, then one.

"One damn cow at a time," Randy swore. "It's taking six guys to get one cow out. Where the hell are they?"

The jubilation Clem had on the first day was completely gone. Now it was just plain hard work. Dexter wrenched his shoulder. Ryan got nicked in the thigh by a struggling cow. Shuckabur, Randy's favorite horse, sprained an ankle. During their few down times, Clem ran ice bags to the bunkhouse and the stables.

As if that wasn't bad enough, on Thursday it started to rain.

Clem first felt the splatter on her face.

"No," she protested. They'd been working for

six days straight and had only made it through about a third of the four hundred.

"Let's move faster. I think we can get the next ones through," Randy called.

"We'll have to get as many cows out as possible before that creek rises. After that, it'll be time to switch to plan B," Ryan answered.

"Which is?" Clem was encouraged that Ryan had a plan B.

"Don't know yet." He shot her a tired smile.

"I'm really hating this," Dexter commented two hours later, as they wrestled a cow into the pen.

Randy, Ryan and the hands took the opportunity for a short coffee break. "We should shoot them," Clem said dully. "I'm so tired that I could just lie down and sleep."

"You aren't going to shoot them." Dexter's face was dark. "It's personal now. I'm not going to be defeated by a few cows."

"A few big cows," Clem corrected him.

"A few big cows," he admitted with a small smile. "You could stay home and rest. No one would blame you. We're more used to this."

Clem shook her head stubbornly. "If you guys are here, then I'm going to be right with you."

"Good for you. We need you." He clasped his hand on her shoulder.

She felt a glow of pride from the steady pressure of his hand.

"Okay, enough of a rest. It's back to the mine," Dexter called.

A collective groan went up as everyone rose from their perches around a small campfire, tossing the remains of their coffee onto the ground. Ryan kicked the fire out.

By late afternoon, the drizzle had turned into a steady downpour. The path was slippery and visibility next to nothing.

"We've got to call this off." Ryan rode up to Dexter. "It's getting too bad. I don't think we'll be able to work again until the storm passes."

Dexter swore.

"It's probably for the best," Clem said. "We can all use the rest. Your shoulder surely could use a day off. We've been working really hard."

"And have hardly made a dent."

Clem smiled. "I have 123 more cows than I had before."

"And I'm going to get you all six hundred if it kills me," Dexter promised through clenched teeth. He rode Calisto to the trailer and unsaddled her with determined movements.

Clem stared after him, unable to keep the worry from her face.

"He's like that when he's working," Ryan assured her. "He hates when things don't go as planned."

THE RANCH HOUSE WAS FILLED with restless tension as the men waited out the storm. They were supposed to be resting, but they pored over the maps, pacing up and down the living room, throwing ideas around.

Clem sat at her father's desk and tried to concentrate on the forms she was supposed to be filling out. But her eyes and her mind kept wandering to Dexter. She watched him stare out the window, as if it was the rain's fault that he was forced indoors.

And she knew that if it weren't for Ryan, they'd be out in the storm working.

Early Sunday morning they were back at the plateau as soon as the rain began to taper off. While the cowboys hadn't appreciated the time off, the dogs and horses sure did. They had an energy and vigor that had been seriously lacking during the days before the rain. Shuckabur was back in full form, not even favoring the sprained ankle. Archie was full of pep, too. Clem could barely hold him, he was so anxious to get to work.

The creek, however, had swollen to twice its previous size. Clem didn't know how they were going to convince anything, much less a feral cow, to plunge into it. But Dexter and Randy didn't seem to have any qualms. Together, they roped the first cow and dragged it toward the creek.

"Is it my imagination, or are these suckers getting bigger?" Ryan asked her.

"I was just thinking the same thing. Look at the horn spread."

"And the bigger they get, the less cooperative they are."

Clem sighed. "Poison?"

Ryan shook his head. "Naw. We'll get 'em out. It looks bad, but that's just because of the weather. Once everything dries up, this will go a lot faster." He sounded hopeful, but Clem knew differently.

As the days turned into weeks, September into late October, it didn't seem to matter how much they discussed alternatives. Each conversation ended with the dismal conclusion that only sheer persistence would win this particular fight. They all agreed that whichever side blinked first would lose. Personally, Clem thought that the cows had the upper hand.

For Clem, it was the little things that frustrated her the most. They ran out of rope so they had to take a special trip to town to buy more. Their rain gear sprang leaks, so they spent an evening patching it. They all came down with head colds. But every time Clem was ready to give up, one of them told her she could do it, *they* could do it.

Finally, they caught a break.

The last week of October, the rain stayed away, the creek lowered, and the cows seemed to be tired of fighting. They were running out of feed and seemed anxious to make it further down the mountain where it wasn't as cold at night.

"Wouldn't it be nice if we found the others had wandered down to the ranch pasture?" Clem asked, her voice wistful.

"If that happens, you should buy a lottery ticket." Dexter laughed. "The good news is we seem to be able to get them through in fives and sixes now. Maybe we took out the leaders already and these guys are ready to give up."

Clem could only hope.

After two days of good weather, their spirits had risen, and Clem's hope paid off when they were able to move over seventy head in an afternoon.

"We're more than halfway," Randy said, nodding. "I think we've got them licked."

"Should we quit for the day?" Ryan squinted up at the sun. "Daylight's running out on us."

"One more?" Randy said. And everyone agreed.

Clem had her job down. She and Archie and two fresh dogs, started to herd two little ones toward the creek. Dexter had three and joined up with her. The cows were finally herding the way they should. A little nip on an ankle and the cows obediently trotted in the right direction.

"You want to switch places with me?" Dexter asked.

She shook her head. "We're almost done. I'm fine."

"Switch with me, anyway," he ordered. "Part of the slope is eroding."

"So you'll fall into the ravine instead of me?" she inquired with a raised eyebrow.

"Don't argue with me," he said.

She nodded. She was too tired to argue. She reined in Archie and let Dexter take the side next to the eroding edge.

"Feel better?" she asked.

He didn't say anything, just watched the cows, making sure they kept going where they were supposed to go. She looked over her shoulder, Ryan and a hand were coming up behind them with another five.

"We'd better move these along a little faster," she said, tightening her thighs around Archie to get him move more quickly. "They're right on our tail."

Dexter glanced over his shoulder and then pushed Calisto into a trot.

"Come on, slowpokes," Ryan called. "You're holding up the train."

Dexter had a few choice words for him.

Ryan just burst into laughter.

"Almost there," Clem said. She could see the plateau as they turned the steep corner. But close as they were, they couldn't let up. This last bit was the worst part of the whole trek. She pushed ahead to make sure the cows went into the portable corral rather than down the hill the way they wanted.

Dexter scooted behind a cow that had decided to stop right in the middle of the path. He nudged it forward.

It refused to move one way or another. A dog nipped its thigh. But all that did was make the cow mad. Dexter roped its horns, trying to tug the cow forward. But it stood as if its hooves were rooted in the dirt beneath it.

Clem's throat closed as the cow began to move backward, twisting and turning in an effort to rid itself of the rope. The other cows became agitated, and in an instant, she found herself pinned to the wall. She yelped as the pressure on her leg increased. She kicked Archie's side, and the horse bolted forward, sending two cows in different directions.

"Behind you!" Ryan hollered.

Clem watched Ryan's herd advance quickly, not caring that Dexter and the furious cow were right in front of them. Dexter struggled as he tried to get the cow under control, but inch by inch the cow kept moving away until it was right on the edge. Then Clem realized that Dexter had made a mistake. He'd wrapped the rope around his forearm, and that meant if the cow went over, *he'd* go over.

CHAPTER NINE

DEXTER WAS FINALLY GETTING the upper hand. The cow bellowed at being caught, wriggling like a prize marlin, using all its weight to try to throw off the offensive rope.

What Dexter would have given for a good old-fashioned dart gun, the kind that could knock a rhino out with one shot in the shoulder.

"Right behind you!" Ryan called.

Dexter swore as he saw the advancing herd in his peripheral vision.

"Let the cow go!" Clem yelled. "Let the cow go."

Dexter tightened his hold. He wasn't going to let go.

WHAT WAS HE DOING? Clem felt tears of fright spring to her eyes. She was going to have to watch him die. Ryan couldn't do anything to help. Dexter and Calisto were on their own. They worked in perfect tandem, muscles tense with the strain, but Ryan's herd was advancing fast.

Clem watched in horror as the cow changed tactics, rather than pulling back, it charged forward, coming very close to clipping Calisto. At the last moment, the horse danced out of the way. The cow charged again, this time forcing Calisto and Dexter closer to the edge. Even though it was a small ravine, a fall from six feet could cause irreparable harm to a man and horse. Brush and hard rocks would be the only things that would break their fall. Finally an idea came to Clem. If she could distract the cow, Dexter would have a better opportunity to tie it down. Clem jabbed her heels into Archie and began to concentrate on fixing another lasso around the cow's horns. Archie didn't have the strength of Calisto, but he could certainly edge the cow toward the trees, away from the ravine.

It didn't even occur to her that she might be hurt as she threw her rope, a perfect loop, and caught the horn of the cow mad enough to take everyone down.

The increased flow and volume of Dexter's cursing indicated the level of his displeasure. Clem just smiled grimly at him, as she focused on the cow. She jerked hard on the rope, but instead of tightening, her perfect—or not so perfect, as it was turning out—loop slipped loose as Archie pulled back. At the lack of resistance, the horse stopped short.

The next thing Clem knew, she was watching Dexter's face freeze as her momentum kept her traveling backward, without the horse. She kicked her boots from the stirrups so she didn't drag Archie down on top of her.

An object in motion stays in motion, until there's something to stop it. Her eleventh-grade physics came back to her as she hurtled toward the ravine, the same ravine she was trying to save Dexter from. Gosh, the sky was blue, the hills green. *Tuck and curl* leapt into her mind before she crashed to the ground. The very hard ground.

"Oomph!"

She felt all the breath leave her body.

Everything went black, except for the stars exploding behind her eyes.

An object at rest stays at rest.

CLEM HADN'T THOUGHT being dead would hurt so damn much.

She also hadn't figured the Grim Reaper would shake her shoulder, pat her face and curse her in such a strangled voice. She'd expected a better bedside manner.

"What the hell did you think you were trying to prove?" It was Dexter's voice, gruff with panic. That meant she wasn't dead.

"Clem. Wake up."

"Can't see." Was that her voice, sounding as if it'd been dragged through a gravel pit?

"Open your eyes," he ordered.

She did as she was told, only to find his bulk blocking her view of the sky. He began to run his hands up and down her body, checking for broken bones.

Ryan skidded down the ravine, his face ragged. "Sorry about that. Is she okay?" He knelt next to Dexter and helped him gently move her limbs.

She tried to raise her head.

A shaking hand pushed her down and placed something against her forehead.

"Don't move until we know the extent of your injuries," Dexter said.

"Archie?" was the only word she could gasp out.

"He's fine. What the hell were you doing?"

Being dead would be better than hearing the disdainful reproof in his voice. Now, not only were her ribs killing her, but her ego throbbed. She tried hard to suck in some air, and found herself shaking with fear. *Suck it up, Clem. Suck it up.*

"Do?" She could hear herself moan, and bit back the sound, making her voice as rough as his, just so she wouldn't cry.

"I was trying to save your ass, Scott." Clem

willed her heart to stop jerking out of her throat and the sharp pain to cease stabbing at her side. Neither paid her any mind. With the greatest effort she had ever exerted, she began to sit up, but a gentle hand on her shoulder, her very sore shoulder, effectively pinned her to the ground.

"Almost done, Clem," Ryan said. "Just be a little more patient."

"Don't move," Dexter ordered. His voice then gentled. "At least until you catch your breath."

"I'm fine," she protested, annoyed that her voice croaked.

"You've just taken a nasty spill, and you've got blood everywhere." He eased the pressure from her forehead and she squinted. "Hold this," he said, and put her hand on the handkerchief. "Where's Randy?"

"He went to bring the truck in closer."

Gingerly Clem tried to sit up again. This time both men just watched her. She felt around her forehead and then tried to move to her knees. Dexter's hand was supporting her back. She welcomed his strength.

"Can you move your feet?"

She wriggled her ankles. No paralysis. That was good. Her shaking had subsided and she felt very cold. Dexter must have sensed that, because he wrapped her in his coat.

He pressed his hands on her ribs.

"Sore?"

"Y-yes."

"That hurt?" He probed her abdomen.

She shook her head.

"Take a deep breath," he ordered.

She sucked in air and he pressed down.

"Any discomfort?"

"No. You sound like a doctor."

"Nope. Just used to injuries. This is part of the job description."

He took the handkerchief from her forehead. "Good, the bleeding's stopped. You might need a stitch or two."

"I think I can ride home," she gasped.

"I don't think so." Dexter smiled down at her.

"I want to stand," she insisted.

Still supporting her back, Dexter helped her to her feet.

Bad idea.

The world tipped back and forth like a seesaw. She teetered backward and Dexter caught her. He lowered her to the ground, and she leaned up against him. Tears slipped from her eyes, and she started to shake again.

Dexter pulled her close.

"Now, none of that crying," he whispered into her hair.

She couldn't stop. She knew it wasn't just the spill that was making her cry. She was crying for the mess her life was in, for her helplessness. She hated the fact she was weak.

"Cowboys don't cry," Dexter said with a smile.

"This one does," she said with a sniff.

"Just stay put, Clem. Rest. Once you get your wind back, you'll be fine." His voice was very close to her ear; she could feel his lips on her temple.

A small rest sounded like a good idea. It would allow her to find the energy to get up and climb up on Archie.

Five minutes later, her tears were dry, and she decided she'd rested long enough. If they hurried, they could probably finish their herding. She furrowed her brow and struggled to break out of Dexter's grasp.

"Don't you ever do a damn thing I say?" Dexter's voice sliced into her, and she moved her head a little to quickly for its liking. The trees whirled around her.

Before they steadied, Ryan was on her other side,

holding a black first aid kit. "Randy's just up the road."

Dexter nodded. "Let's try to get you standing. It might hurt a little bit. Let us know if there's a lot of discomfort."

Clem protested. "No, I can stand. Let me try. What about the cows?"

But before she could make herself obey, she was lifted to her feet. The trees moved up and down, and she felt as if she was going to throw up. Dexter put one strong hand on her elbow, the other on the small of her back. Then he moved her to stand against the bank of the ravine.

"I want to put something on that cut," Dexter told Ryan, as he took the first aid kit and began to rummage through it. "The cows are fine," he reassured her, "You hired good men."

Clem was relieved.

Ryan frowned. "It might be better to get an ambulance out here for her."

"We can get her to the hospital quicker than the ambulance," Dexter said. "It would take them a while to even find us."

"There's no need for the hospital," Clem said, annoyed that her teeth were chattering.

"Shock's making you feel cold," he told her. "Just concentrate on breathing."

"It doesn't hurt that much," she lied. "I just got the wind knocked out of me. Where's Ryan going?"

"He's going to find out where Randy is with that damn truck."

Some gravel fell on her head and she looked up to see Archie on the edge of the ravine, staring down at her. More loose rock came down, but she ignored it.

"You could at least thank me," she muttered.

"For what?" Dexter looked amused. He flexed his wrist. "I damn near broke my arm trying to hold on to that cow." He ripped open an antiseptic towelette. "Here, hold this."

"I'm fine," Clem insisted, but she held out her hand as he draped the towelette on it. He pulled out another hanky and poured water from his canteen on it.

"What happened to the cow?" Clem asked, wincing as he did a gross-scale rinse of her forehead. "You have to let it go?" She knew she sounded wistful.

"It was either the cow or you. I guess I'd rather have you. Ryan caught it farther down."

Clem smiled against her will and then winced as he dabbed none too gently at her cut with the antiseptic. It hurt enough to send stinging prickles shooting down the back of her neck.

"Hey!" Clem protested. "You're making it hurt on purpose."

"You've got debris embedded in there." He studied the wound, so close she could feel his breath on her cheek. "You're definitely going to need stitches. But these should help."

He pulled out a set of butterfly bandages and applied them with the hand of an experienced healer.

"You do that well."

"You learn if you're the only one to do it." He nodded at his handiwork. "That should keep you until we get you to the hospital."

"I don't think so."

"This isn't something we're going to debate. I want an X ray of those ribs."

Clem was silent. Suddenly she didn't have the energy to argue. She closed her eyes.

Dexter gently shook her. "Clem. Don't go to sleep."

"I'm not going to sleep."

"Open your eyes."

She opened the one that wasn't starting to swell shut. "It's too bright."

He transferred his hat onto her head, but she still had the overwhelming urge to sleep.

"Clem, did I tell you about the time that Randy and Ryan tied me up to a cactus buck-naked?"

Her good eye popped open and she giggled. "Really?"

"No, but I thought that would wake you up."

"You'd have been picking stickers out for weeks," she murmured.

"Clem, don't go to sleep. Stay awake. For me, please."

She heard footsteps, then Ryan said something about a concussion.

She peered at him. "No concussion. Tired."

"I know you're tired. But stay awake until we get you to the hospital."

"Just a nap."

"No."

"Walk?"

"If it'll keep you awake."

"Okay," Clem said, and yawned. She tried to move off the bank. If Dexter's hand hadn't been right under her elbow, she would have fallen down, her legs seeming incapable to support her.

"I don't think so." Doubt filled his eyes.

"Let's get to the road," she suggested, and yawned again. "Ow, my head hurts."

He didn't smile.

She wobbled toward a slight slope that would

take her out of the ravine to where Archie was nibbling on grass. He didn't look remorseful at all.

She bent over to clamber up and winced.

''Hell.'' Dexter muttered, and with the ease of a weight lifter, scooped her off the ground in a movement so quick she only knew what he was doing when the world swirled around her. He'd easily got them both up to the bank, carrying her the few yards to the road.

She pressed her lips together, her ribs aching.

''You look like you're going to pass out,'' Dexter observed. He didn't let go of her.

''I'm not going to pass out.'' She tried to make her voice stronger, but she couldn't. ''I'm really tired.''

''I still don't know what the hell you were trying to do.'' The edge of his voice caught her consciousness and she realized that she had drifted again.

''Oh,'' Clem observed. ''I suppose you'd rather I had just let you go over.''

He couldn't know the cost of those words, but he seemed to be heartened by the fact that she was still feisty.

''I *wasn't* going to go over, until you came barreling in like the cavalry,'' he said mildly. ''Jeez, Clem. I told you to stay out of my way. I know what I'm doing and you don't.''

Dexter's tone, his fright, worked their way into her consciousness. With great effort, she struggled to stay awake.

"Look," she said, trying as hard as she could not to gasp with each breath. "I'm sorry. I thought you were about to go down the ravine."

They sat in silence. Dexter's hold on her never loosened.

Finally, he said, "You scared the hell out of me. When you went over, I didn't know what I was going to find."

"I'm fine."

Clem felt strong hands lift her into the truck. She tried to sit up, but found that leaning against Dexter was much more comfortable. She could feel his chin resting on her head. And as hard as she tried to stay conscious, the rumbling of the masculine voices had a lulling effect on her.

"Horses?" she asked suddenly.

"Ryan's going to take them back."

"Oh."

She felt a shake, and far away heard Dexter command, "Stay awake."

"Then talk to me," Clem said. "Tell me about yourself. I promise to stay awake."

SO DEXTER SCOTT TALKED. He found himself talking more than he'd ever talked in his life. He told

Clem about meeting Ben Thorton and how much he missed working with him. He told her about Randy and Ryan. He talked and talked and talked. Clem asked questions here and there just to let him know she was listening and he knew what an effort it was. His throat was sore when they arrived at the emergency room.

DEXTER SAT IN THE WAITING room. He hated hospitals more than he hated walking. The antiseptic smell was overwhelming. The hospital personnel had swept Clem away and told him to wait. He glanced at his watch. He'd been waiting nearly two hours.

Randy had gone back to the ranch to put up the horses and the dogs.

He jammed his hat deeper on his head and pretended to read a magazine. Every fifteen minutes, he inquired at the desk. "Any news about Clementine Wells?"

The nurse looked at him sympathetically. "When we know something, we'll tell you."

"They're going to do X rays of her ribs, right?"

"I don't know what the doctor has decided to do, sir. Have you notified her closest relatives?"

He shook his head. "Is it that bad?"

The nurse was evasive. "You might want to contact them."

With his heart in his throat, Dexter drove back to the ranch house. There wasn't much he did know about Clem's condition, but one thing was for certain—her cow-chasing days were over. He'd already buried one. He wasn't going to bury another. He rifled through the desk, looking for a phone number for her parents. He didn't even know their names.

He didn't find anything, but he remembered there was a notepad by the phone. He went to the kitchen and saw that he'd guessed right.

His fingers trembled as he dialed the number. The phone rang once, twice.

"Hello?" a female asked.

"Mrs. Wells?" He could barely speak.

"Yes?"

"My name is Dexter Scott. I'm sorry to call you, but your daughter Clem's been in an accident."

CLEM'S HEAD THROBBED AS IF someone was pounding on it with a rubber mallet. She opened one eye and couldn't place herself. It took a minute for her to understand that she was in a hospital room.

She tried to sit up and groaned, her hand coming up to her head, where she felt a bandage.

"Hi."

The voice startled her and she turned to find its speaker, but before she could, the room began to swing around her.

"Whoa." Was that her voice? She sounded like a toad.

When she opened her eyes again, Dexter stood over her, his face ashen. He looked as if he hadn't slept in a long time.

"Hi," he repeated as he bestowed a sweet smile on her. "It's about time you woke up."

"What time?"

"About ten o'clock in the morning."

"Morning? Where are the cows?"

"Where we left them, I imagine." He sat down next to her. "Water?"

She nodded. He stuck a straw into a plastic cup and brought it to her mouth.

She sipped and then lay back down. "You look awful," she said.

"You look worse."

There was a long silence.

"Archie?" Clem asked.

"He's fine. Taking the day off."

Day off. Clem stared at Dexter. "Where is everyone else?"

"They're working."

"You're not working."

"No," he said. "I'm not. I needed to know that you're going to be okay."

"Am I going to be okay?"

He nodded with a grim smile. "Bumps, bruised ribs. X ray came out fine, no internal injuries. That was what we were really worried about, and the concussion. Plus you've got quite a shiner."

"Concussion? I don't remember hitting my head."

"That's the reason you're here. They wanted to make sure you'd be able to wake up."

"When can I leave?" She looked down and realized she was in a standard-issue hospital gown.

"Maybe this afternoon, depending on how you feel. Your folks should be here by then."

Clem struggled to sit up. "What?"

"Your parents."

"My parents?"

"Yes."

She fell back against the pillows. "Please tell me you didn't call my parents." She reached for her locket. It wasn't there.

"I did," Dexter said quietly. "I thought they should know."

"It was just a little spill." She tried to change the subject. "Did you take my locket?"

"It was a little more than a spill, and I thought it would be prudent for your parents to know." He paused. "I didn't see your locket."

Clem was overwhelmed by contradicting feelings. Loss of her locket battled with deep resentment that Dexter had called her parents. He couldn't know how hard it was for her to be independent around her parents. "I wish you hadn't."

Dexter's voice was hard. "Well, I did. Deal with it."

CLEMENTINE LEANED FORWARD as Claire ran a comb through her hair. She'd had mixed feelings seeing her mother's still-smooth face in the hospital room's doorway. She hadn't been able to hold back the tears, and Claire had rushed to hug her, giving Clem the comfort that only a mother can offer. But Clem had known there was an enormous cost for that comfort. With each moment Claire's arms had been around her, Clementine had felt herself losing control of her life. Her mother had brought with her fresh clothes from the ranch. Pink, no less. Clem had frowned at the color.

"It was in your closet," Claire had said, her voice dry. "I was in a hurry. What can I say?"

"Pink?"

"Oh, it's just until you get home."

Claire tugged on a snarl, and the room tilted. Clem was relieved that the doctor said her vertigo would probably disappear in a day or two.

"I can do my own hair, Mom," Clementine said wryly, feeling like she was six years old.

"I know that, honey. Humor your old mother. Let me fuss over you. You had us all very worried."

"It was just a little tumble," Clem muttered, watching her mother open a bobby pin with her mouth, then jab it into Clem's hair to keep it out of her face. Clem didn't even have the energy to protest.

"A concussion and a set of bruised ribs is more than a little tumble." Her mother's voice was concerned.

"When am I being released?"

"Your dad's arranging that now."

"Where's Dexter?"

"That nice young man who called us? The poor boy seemed out of his mind with worry for you."

Clem pressed her lips together. She didn't want him to be out of his mind with worry. She wanted him to be here. She wanted to be wearing something other than pink and not have bobby pins in her hair.

"Where is he?"

"He said something about going back to work.

He wanted to get something done before it got dark."

Clem couldn't help but feel a little deserted.

"We've worked so hard with those cows," she said after a while.

"That's what I'm told."

Her father walked in the room and bestowed a gentle kiss on the only part of Clem's forehead that wasn't visibly bruised. Jim Wells was a very good-looking man and aging even better. A thick mane of white hair and a face creased from too many days in the sun were the only things that revealed Jim Wells's age.

"What are you doing here, Dad? I wasn't expecting you until Thanksgiving."

"We couldn't not come once we got the phone call." Jim Wells gave her a charming smile that in the past had gentled the toughest horse or the orneriest cow. "You're going to need someone to help now that you're out of commission. You'll be able to sleep in your own bed and get the rest you need."

"I'm okay," Clem said, but the thought of sitting back and letting her father do the job was beginning to tempt.

"You took quite a spill," her mother observed.

"It wasn't that bad," Clem muttered. "Dad?"

"Yes, honey?"

"I lost my locket."

"That's okay. I'll get you a new one."

"It must have come off when I fell."

"Don't worry about it. Everything is going to be all right. You're going to be just fine."

But Clem wasn't too sure about that.

She hated how relieved she was that her father was here. She hadn't wanted Dex to call her parents—not because of what they'd do, but because of her own desire to relinquish all control, to have her father just make everything right again. Jim Wells was used to working with men like Dexter, Randy and Ryan. If she knew her father, he'd be treating them like the sons he'd never had before the day was out.

She would never be missed.

CHAPTER TEN

IT WAS COMFORTING to be in her own bed with her mother fussing over her. Just as Clementine had predicted, her father stepped into her place, filling her spot on the team as easily as if he'd been an original member. In the mornings, she heard the cowboys hitching up the trailers, loading the saddles and the dogs. With Jim Wells back, many of the hired men had decided to stay on at the bunkhouse until the job had ended, and Claire had her hands full trying to cook for the crew. At first, because of her vertigo, Clem wasn't much of a help, but as the days wore on, she began to feel stronger and stronger and more able to assist her mother.

Clem found immense comfort in the rhythm and the safety of the kitchen. Unless one of the ovens blew up, she knew her chances for survival were better in the kitchen than on the trail.

"I'm glad you're here," Clem said as her mother handed her the corn bread batter to spread into the pans. Cowchip hovered beside her, looking for a morsel or two to drop to the ground. Now that Claire was back, Cowchip followed her everywhere.

"I certainly didn't expect to be put to work so quickly," Claire laughed. "But it reminds me of old times. It's good for your father, too. He likes being around the young men. Good thing there are two of us. It makes the cooking that much easier."

They worked together in companionable silence.

"I like your young man."

"My young man?" Clem looked at her mother in surprise.

"Dexter."

Clem flushed. "He's not my young man."

"He sure watches over you as if he is."

"I'm not ready for anything like that. I already made one mistake, I'm not eager to make another one." Clem wiped the edges of the pans, then popped them in the oven before taking the bowl to the sink. Clem hadn't seen much of Dexter since her accident, though he did drop in every evening, at first with reports on their progress. The news wasn't as encouraging as she wanted, but for the past few nights, his visits had been purely social. Even when she asked about the cows, he only gave her the briefest amount of information. It was as if the roundup had nothing to do with her.

"The carrots need to be stripped."

Clem nodded and rummaged through the refrigerator to find the ten-pound bag of carrots. "I appreciate your going shopping."

"What else were we going to feed everyone?" Claire asked.

Clem started peeling and slicing the carrots. She liked cooking. She was good at it. It didn't really bother her that she'd been left out of the men's work. What in the world made her think she should be out riding with them, anyway?

"Dexter isn't like Nick," Claire said suddenly, picking up their earlier conversational thread.

Clem nodded, only half listening. She peeled more carrots. "But he doesn't talk."

"Still waters run deep," her mother quoted. "He seems to say plenty to you."

"I suppose."

"He seems to understand your needs, too."

"Maybe."

"So when are you going to go out with them again?" Claire asked gently. "I hear Archie's getting mighty restless being left behind all the time."

Clem kept on peeling carrots. She didn't want to look up. "My ribs still ache pretty badly."

"Really?" Her mother cocked her head to the side.

Clem flushed. Her mother could always see right through her.

"Well, they're better than they were."

"I would think you'd want to participate. It seems as if the hard stuff's been taken care of. Now it's just the herding."

Clem laughed. "With these cows, it's the herding that's hard."

"Still, you don't want to miss out on the fun."

Clem brought half the carrots over to the stove. "You need help here."

"Heavens, I've cooked for twice as many with less notice," Claire said. "I'll just start earlier."

Clem didn't say anything. "I've got paperwork I should get done."

Her mother clicked her tongue. "Clem, you can do the paperwork anytime. It's not every day that you get to learn from cowboys who have this much experience. I would've thought you'd be itching to get out there. Count your booty."

"I'll count them when they get in our pasture."

Claire stopped what she was doing. "Clem, I didn't raise a quitter."

"You also didn't raise a fool," Clem retorted.

"And how would going out and getting your cows make you a fool?"

Clem wasn't sure how to explain what she felt to

her mother. Finally, in frustration, she said, "I can't keep up!"

"What does that mean?"

"Mom, you should see how good they are. They seem very casual about it, but they're truly the best in the world. I just slow them down."

Claire frowned. She pushed her silver hair off her forehead. "It doesn't seem to me that any of those boys hold the impression you slowed them down even one iota."

"We lost cows and time the day I fell."

"Any other person could have fallen. That much they made clear to me. You were just in the wrong place at the wrong time," her mother countered.

Clem shook her head. "They've got plenty of help with Dad out there. There really isn't much to miss. It's a lot safer here." Clem couldn't understand why tears were welling up in her eyes.

"Safe isn't always better, honey," Claire said.

"I know, Mom." Clem sniffed back her tears and started to rip up lettuce for salad. "But I think that's the only way I can handle things."

"No!" Her mother was vehement. "You're bigger than that. Clem, there's only one life. And when it's done and over, will you be someone who played it safe and got nothing or someone who risked it all and got everything?"

Clem couldn't answer.

Her mother took the head of lettuce out of Clem's hands and wrapped her in a tight hug.

"It's been a hard year, but you're stronger. Just look at what you've done."

Clem allowed herself to feel the comfort of her mother's hug before she pulled away. "Thanks, but there are plenty of other risks I can take. I don't need this one."

Her mother sighed. "If you think staying here is for the best, I won't argue anymore."

Clem nodded. "Yes. I think it is."

THE MEN CAME BACK HOME tired. The day hadn't gone as smoothly as planned.

"I thought that we'd be done by now," Ryan muttered.

"It's just slow work. We'll have them in before the end of the week," Jim Wells said encouragingly. "Look, we've already got three hundred fifty. You boys do good work."

"It's not the same without Clem," Randy said suddenly. He gave her a friendly smile as she offered him a plate of spiced carrots. "When are you going to help us?"

"It's only been a couple of days since she's really been back on her feet," Dexter objected.

"But she's a toughie," Randy remarked. "Aren't you, Clem?"

Jim cleared his throat. "Clem took quite a tumble. We can hardly blame her if she wants to sit out a few innings to catch her breath."

"As long as it's just a few innings." Randy stared at her pointedly. "We could use the extra hand."

"I thought Dad was filling my shoes just fine," Clem joked.

"And then some," Jim Wells agreed as he patted his stomach. "Claire, the food is delicious."

"Thank Clem," her mother said smoothly. "She did half the cooking."

"She can cook," Ryan agreed. "Almost as good as she can ride."

Clem laughed. "That's very nice of you, but I think I should stick with the cooking rather than the riding."

"You can't," Randy persisted. "You're too damn good to be stuck at home cooking." He glanced in Claire's direction. "No offense, Mrs. Wells."

"None taken," Claire said. "I agree with you."

"Clem's a sane adult," Dexter said again. "If she wants to go, she'll go. If she doesn't, we should respect that."

"You would say that, Scott." The bitterness and impatience in Randy's voice surprised Clem.

"And what would you mean by that, Miller?" Dexter dropped his fork and stared at his friend.

"You want her to take the safe route, just like Joanna."

"Randy." Ryan put his hand on his brother's shoulder.

"I'll pretend you didn't say that," Dexter said through clenched teeth, then started eating again.

"The way you want to pretend that Clem would be better off at home? Man, that's a bunch of bull. You know that Clem was *born* for this life."

"But if she doesn't want it," Dexter said, keeping his voice even, but the death grip he had on his fork belied his calm, "then she should be allowed to make up her own mind."

"She's scared, damn it. Everybody gets scared. But she's got to get past it."

"Stop it!" Clem stood up and slammed her hands down on the table, making her ribs throb in protest. The blood was rushing through her head so loudly she couldn't hear herself think. "Would you stop talking about me as if I'm not here? I can make my own decisions. And if I want to go, I'll go. But right now, my ribs hurt and I don't want to. Okay?"

She sat down again and the table fell into stunned silence.

After a beat, Jim Wells ventured, "So anybody been following the 49ers?"

Ryan picked up Clem's father's cue and the talk turned to football and the great season that the 49ers were having.

A few moments later Clem started to clear the table.

She was running water into the sink when Randy came up with a pile of dishes.

"I'm sorry, Clem," he said as he put the dishes in the sink.

She watched the suds separate and rise.

"Don't be, you're entitled to your opinion."

"It's not just my opinion," Randy said. "It's something that I know in my gut. You need to be out there with us. You need to be watching what we're doing."

"If it was just watching, that'd be okay. But I know I'd end up doing and that's when I get hurt."

"Got hurt. Once."

"And what if it happens again?" She was going to cry again.

"Then it happens again. But you can't do what Dex did and just close up because you're afraid of the pain. You'll never live a full life that way."

"How can you say that after what happened to Joanna?"

Randy's eyes were more serious than she'd ever seen them before. "I can say that *because* of Joanna. You'd have really liked her. She wasn't like Dex at all. She was happy, she talked a mile a minute, and she was full of life. I loved her."

"But she died."

He nodded. "I think about Joanna every day. Every time I pass a family, I wonder how many kids we'd have by now. We both wanted a bunch. Joanna really did live every day like it was the last. She squeezed every moment of joy and excitement out of life she could. It was exhausting just keeping up with her."

Clem inhaled. "She was a braver soul than I am."

Randy shook his head. "I don't think so. She had a lot of fear. But what was beautiful about Joanna was that she didn't let the fear keep her from doing what she wanted to do. She just shoved it aside and walked forward."

It's all about moving forward.

Jim Wells's words echoed in Clem's mind.

"Sorry. I didn't mean to beat a dead horse. But I want you back on Archie by the end of the week.

You're really that good.'' His lecture ended, Randy left the kitchen.

Clem finished the dishes by herself.

DEXTER FOUND IT HARD to concentrate on the short debriefing session. He wondered what Randy and Clem had talked about. He'd warned Randy about pushing her too hard. Clem wasn't Joanna. She didn't have the streak of recklessness that had led to Joanna's demise. He was glad when Ryan yawned and rolled up his maps.

''Man, I am exhausted,'' Ryan commented. ''I can't wait to get the rest of those cows out. Then I can look for the others.'' Ryan nodded to Clem. '''Night, Clem.''

Randy joined him, settling his hat on his head. ''Come on out with us tomorrow, Clem. No hard work, just to watch.''

Clem didn't reply, instead she tugged on Dexter's sleeve as he started to follow the Millers out the door.

''Can I talk to you?'' she asked.

Dexter studied her face. It had begun to heal, but he wasn't so certain that she should go out tomorrow, even to watch. They were doing a fine job of getting the cows from the canyon. Even though it was going a lot slower than anyone had expected, the four hundred cows would be safely on their way to market in a matter of days. Then they'd concentrate on the missing two hundred. Like a dog on a trail, Ryan wasn't about to be defeated. He was going to find them.

Ryan and Jim Wells had seemed to hit it off right at the beginning, and Dexter noticed the two often rode together. Dexter wasn't certain Jim Wells was up to the physicality of the work, but he supposed that the rancher wouldn't push past his limits. He wasn't so sure about Clem, though, which was why he'd feel much better if Clem just sat out these last few rounds.

"Sure."

He followed Clem to the staircase and watched as she sat down at the bottom step. She gazed out the window at the pitch-black valley that surrounded the house. Dexter leaned up against the railing of the stairs and waited for her to say what she wanted to say.

"No matter what Randy says, I'm not going with you," she finally admitted.

Relief coursed through Dexter. Now he didn't have to persuade her otherwise.

Unexpectedly he found himself asking, "What made you come to that decision?"

Clem didn't say anything for a long time. Finally,

she cleared her throat and gave a small shrug with her slim shoulders. "I just can't do it."

Dexter looked out the window as his relief at her decision evaporated. Any answer would have been better than that. She didn't like the life. She hated ranching. She hated horses. But not *I just can't do it.*

"I just can't do it, Dex." Joanna stared at him, her eyes filling up with tears. "And you're mean for making me. You know how scared I am."

"All riders fall off their horses." Dexter's patience was at its end. "We don't have any choice, Jo. I need you if we're going to get these cows in. You're our fourth man."

"I'm not a man. I'm a girl."

Dexter snorted. "You're fourteen. If you're big enough to have your own horse, you're big enough to work for its keep."

"I hate you!"

"Shut up and get on the damn horse! Or I'm going to sell it. I swear, I'll sell him in a heartbeat. Old man Hodges said he thought he'd make mighty fine dog meat."

"I hate you!" Joanna repeated, but Dexter noticed that even though she was screaming and crying, she was getting back on the horse. Before long she was riding. Then, she was smiling.

"Surely there's got to be a better reason than that," Dexter probed.

Clem's lips tightened. She looked up at him, her chin resting on her knee, then stared out at the darkness. She shook her head. "No. There's not. I know my limit. I've reached it. You guys enjoy that thrill. I hate it."

"Do you hate all of it?" Dexter knew he should leave things alone. He should accept her answer and then walk away, rather than trying to find out what had caused her change of mind. The spill had been a bad one, true, but nothing more than a few bruised ribs.

"I hated the hospital. I hated the fact you had to call my parents."

So that was it.

"I thought they needed to know. I'm not blind. They adore you."

"Maybe that's the problem." The bitterness in her voice surprised him.

"What's the problem?"

"I've had a good life. And I should be grateful for it and not try and push the boundaries."

Dexter sat down next to her.

"I might have let you go on believing that if I didn't know you're good at what you do."

''Falling off horses?'' Clem's lips twisted into a smile.

''Riding.''

Clem was silent.

''I think Randy's right,'' Dex admitted against his will. ''I think you should go.''

''But you won't think less of me if I decided not to?''

Dexter thought for a long time. Finally, he said, ''Of course not. There's very little that you could do that would make me think less of you.''

CLEM FELT RELIEF FLOOD through her. ''I thought you might feel like Randy does.''

''Well.'' Dexter seemed to be measuring his words. ''You'd want to get back there eventually. Don't you think?''

She shrugged. ''I don't think so. I think this whole fiasco has taught me I'm just not cut out for this kind of life. When this is over, I'll join my parents in Arizona. I can got back to college, pick up the courses I need to get my degree. There are plenty of jobs that I can do.''

Dexter was silent. Finally, he cleared his throat. ''Is that what you really want?''

Clem bit her lip. ''I'm not sure what I want.''

The silence extended into two minutes.

Finally, Dexter cleared his throat. "Can I say something?"

"Okay." Clem wasn't sure she wanted him to, though.

"I think," he started slowly. "I think, you're feeling sorry for yourself. I think instead of digging in, you're giving up."

Clem's face grew hot.

"I thought you of all people would understand," she retorted.

"Me?" he asked. His eyes glittered, as if he was bracing himself for what she had to say to him. "Why do you say that?"

"What makes you think I'm feeling sorry for myself? Can't everyone just understand that I don't want to go out?"

"Everyone gets frightened sometimes."

"I'm not scared. I simply don't want to go. Can't you understand that?" Clem stood up. "Do you ever think about the fact that Joanna would be alive if on that one day she'd decided not to go out?"

Clem regretted her words when she saw his face. All the color had drained from it.

"I'm sorry, Dexter. I didn't mean to—"

"Yes, Clem," he said, his voice a hard staccato. "Every morning when I get up I wonder what I could have done to prevent Joanna from dying. And if she'd decided not to go out, she would still be alive."

Then he swallowed hard and started to leave.

She reached a hand out and held on. "Don't go, Dexter. Talk to me."

He stopped but wouldn't look at her.

"What happened?"

"I killed her, Clem."

Her throat was dry. She took his hands in hers and squeezed as hard as she could. "No, Dex. It was an accident."

He shook his head. "No. I killed her."

"How can you think that?" Clem wanted to shake him. "It wasn't your fault."

"I've never told anyone this. No one," he whispered.

"What?"

"She didn't want to go."

Clem could barely hear the words. "What?" She bent her head close to his.

"She didn't want to go." The words came out flat, toneless. He cleared his throat. "She didn't want to go."

"But I thought she was having a good time." Clem made her voice as soothing as she could.

"She always did once she got out, but she never wanted to go." Dexter gave a short laugh, his mind left in the past. "I always had to push her out the door."

"So you did it that time?"

His eyes were dry with unshed tears. "Yes. She wasn't feeling well. She had her period and she wanted to stay home. But I bugged her until she went."

"Did she have to go?" Clem asked.

Dexter nodded. "I needed her. She was a good hand, plus I knew Randy wanted to get her alone so he could ask her to marry him."

"Then she couldn't have stayed home."

"Randy could have asked her to marry him at home. Hell, he could have gotten home a little early or taken her out behind the barn after dinner. He didn't have to do it while we were working. But he wanted to."

"So she never knew Randy was going to propose? That he wanted to marry her?" Clem found that inexplicably sad.

Dexter shrugged. "Joanna was a highly intuitive person. I think she knew it was only a matter of time. Randy was hooked. But no, she didn't know it was going to be that day." He pressed his lips tightly together. "I killed her, Clem."

Clem shook her head, tears forming in her eyes. "No, you didn't. You did what you needed to do.

You couldn't have known. No one could have known.'' A tear fell and dropped on his arm.

He looked at it in surprise. ''Why are you crying?''

''Because you can't,'' Clem said with a helpless laugh. ''I'm crying your tears.''

DEXTER PUT A GENTLE HAND on Clem's face and traced the scar in her eyebrow where the stitches had just been taken out. He'd never seen such a beautiful woman in his life, red, puffy eyes and all. ''No one's ever done that for me,'' he said quietly.

Clem brushed away her tears. ''It's just so sad. I'm so sorry that Joanna never knew she was about to be engaged.''

''She knew. I think deep down she knew.''

''Do you think she knew she was going to die?'' Clem asked.

Dexter shook his head. ''I don't think so. I hope not. I hope it was a complete surprise to her.''

Clem wrapped her arms around his neck and she kissed his cheek. He could feel her tears on his face and he hugged her close.

''You don't have to go, Clem,'' he whispered. ''I'll respect whatever decision you make. We all will.''

She sniffed. "Thank you." She looked around. "Do you happen to have another hankie on you?"

He fished it out of his back pocket. "I'm going to need to stock up on these."

"I've washed the others," Clem hiccuped.

He put his arm around her as she blew her nose.

She gave him a watery smile.

"See?" she said. "That's growth."

"What?"

"You're able to just let me cry."

"Since you're crying my tears, I thought it might be for the best."

She laughed.

"You are beautiful," he said, wondering where all his breath had gone.

She looked down at the handkerchief in her hands.

He kissed her cheek and she closed her eyes.

CLEM COULD FEEL THE WARMTH of his breath on her temple, then her ear, and then the nape of her neck. His hands went through her hair and he leaned in for a kiss. It was just a bare brush against her lips.

She moaned in protest as he pulled away. But he wasn't gone for long, as he settled his lips on hers more thoroughly. Clem felt heady as she moved closer. But almost before the kiss had started, it was over. This time he pulled away for good.

"I've got to go."

She shook her head. "You don't have to go."

He nodded with a small smile. "Yes, I do."

She held out her hand to him and indicated the stairs behind her. "Come with me."

He gave her quick peck on her forehead. "As tempting as your offer is, I'm very aware that I'm in your parents' house, with your parents upstairs."

She frowned. "They don't care."

"I care. I care too much about what they think of me to do anything that would—"

Clem smiled. "I'm thirty-two, not eighteen. My virtue would hardly be compromised." Still, she was touched by the reluctance in his face, the regret in the second kiss he placed on her forehead.

He shook his head. "We'll save it for later—once the cows are in. We have a lot to talk about."

She smiled as he walked out.

They *did* have a lot to talk about.

CHAPTER ELEVEN

CLEM COULD ONLY PICK at her food, but the others at the table were feeling triumphant. As her father had predicted, they'd brought in the magic four hundred, and Ryan was already on the trail of the other two hundred. They'd put in a good week's worth of work. Clem knew because she watched their comings and goings from the porch.

Randy always motioned for her to join them, but she'd shaken her head and patted her ribs. The truth was that her body had healed a lot quicker than her mind. She could barely feel her injuries, and her face had just a shadow of a bruise. She'd have a permanent scar on her eyebrow, though, where the doctor had put in six stitches.

"I think we're close to finding that smaller herd. Your dad, here, had some good ideas where to look," Ryan was saying, bringing her back to the conversation.

"I am ready for a long night's sleep," Jim Wells declared. "You young fellows are ready to go party, I know, but I'm ready to collapse. I haven't worked this hard in years. Don't know where you get the stamina, day after day.''

Claire shook her head. ''I warned you about trying to keep up.''

''Oh, he kept up, Mrs. Wells,'' Randy said. ''He even outdid us a couple of times. I think he prevented a stampede this morning. We also know we're almost done and that makes us move a little faster.''

Clem forced herself to smile. She knew what her father was feeling; the excitement of being part of such a knowledgeable crew was heady. She'd felt it right up until the moment she went into the ravine. She wouldn't ever do anything to put herself in that position again.

Claire Wells began to clear the table.

Clem stood up and took the dishes from her mother's hands. ''Don't do that. I think you're going to have to help Dad up those stairs,'' she said, throwing a teasing glance at her dad.

''Oh, no.'' Her mother put her hands on her hips and stared with affection at her husband. ''If he can ride with the cowboys, he can climb his own stairs.''

''But I can't run my own bath,'' he hinted to his wife.

''A grown man and he can't get himself into the tub.''

"I can get myself in the tub," Jim corrected her. With a sidelong look at the cowboys, he grinned as he reached out and patted Claire Wells's bottom. "I just want a shot at getting you in there with me."

Claire laughed and pulled herself out of his grasp. "In front of the children!"

Jim grinned and stood up suddenly, then groaned. Claire became concerned and slipped her shoulder under his arm. "Come on, old man. Let's get you out of here while you still have your dignity left."

They all watched her mother help her father. Clem smiled when Jim goosed Claire halfway up the stairs.

Ryan began to help Clem clear the table.

"So, Clem," Randy said after her parents were out of sight. "When are you going to get out there with us again?"

Clem shook her head with a wry smile. She leaned over the table to gather up the salad bowls. "I think my cowboy days are over. I'll tend to the home fires while you men do the work. Don't you think the supper was good?"

"Excellent," Ryan put in.

Randy stared hard at her and she began to squirm. "Don't tell me that little spill made you chicken or something."

Clem stiffened, but then remembered the talk

she'd had with Dexter. He agreed with her decision. In fact, he seemed relieved.

"Lay off," Dexter growled.

Clem covered her discomfort by clucking. "I'm so chicken that you could fry me up for a Fourth of July picnic."

"Haven't you ever heard of getting back on the horse that threw you?" Randy asked, his tone serious. "Everyone takes spills."

"It wasn't just the spill," Clem said, wondering why he wasn't accepting her explanation as easily as Dexter had. "It just made me realize that I was *am* really out of my league."

Randy rolled his eyes. "Excuses, excuses."

"Miller, that's enough," Dexter said. "If Clem doesn't want to go out, she doesn't have to."

"But that's just the problem, Dex. I think she wants to but is too scared."

Clem didn't like that he echoed her mother's words, but she agreed with him, anyway. "You're right. I am scared. But I'm also smart and I know that I would just slow you all down."

Randy pushed his plate aside. "That's bull. Tell her, Dex. Tell her that she's shoveling it faster than the cows can make it."

"I'm not going to tell her anything," Dex said. "She knows what I think."

Clem noticed he wouldn't look at her, but that

didn't matter. She *did* know what he thought. Now that her father was back, he could take her place and there wasn't much more to discuss. Despite this evening's fatigue Clem could tell how good the exercise was for her father. It had also given him a lot of fun.

She cleared her throat. "Dex and I talked and we agreed that it would probably be safer if I stayed behind."

"Really, now." Randy eyed Dexter. "And whose idea was that, exactly?"

Clem didn't understand the exchange that was going on. She saw Ryan shake his head slightly at Randy, but Randy ignored him and waited for her answer.

"Was it yours, Scott?" The words shot across the table to Dexter, who didn't flinch.

He just stared down Randy.

"No!" Clem jumped to Dexter's defense. "It wasn't his suggestion. I made it, and he agreed. I think it's for the best."

Randy opened his mouth, but then shut it. He threw his napkin on the table and walked out.

Ryan started to clear the table. "He'll get over it," he assured her. "But, Clem, I think he's right. I think you should get in there for this hunt. They're the last, and if they are where we think they are, it's going to be a piece of cake getting them in."

"If it's a piece of cake," Clem said, her voice tart, "then you can do it just fine without me."

"Sure we could." Ryan gave her a full smile. "But it's a lot more fun with you." He shot a sidelong look at Dexter who was staring at the wall. "Dexter behaves a lot better when you're around."

RANDY WAS SITTING on the bunk when Dexter entered the room.

"What do you want?" Randy's voice was rude.

"I want to know why you won't lay off Clem," Dexter said mildly. "If she doesn't want to go, she doesn't want to go."

Randy's eyes glittered, his emotions barely controlled. "Especially since that's what you want, too, right?"

"What do you mean by that?" Dexter felt himself become more defensive. He didn't like the fact that he and Randy seemed to be arguing a lot these days. It seemed as if all the hurt and anger that had been buried after Joanna's death was destined to resurface here at the Wellses' ranch.

Randy stood up and poked Dexter in the chest. "I mean you'd be happy if Clem were just half a woman."

Dexter looked down at the finger in his chest. "If you want to keep that finger, I suggest you remove it. You'd have a heck a time drawing with four fingers.''

Randy didn't laugh. His voice was bitter. ''You're using your fear to cripple her as much as if you broke her leg.''

''What is this about?'' Dexter asked. ''Is this about Clem? If it is, I think it's really none of your business.''

''I'm not going to watch you do that to her.''

''Do what?''

''Encourage her fear.''

''I'm not encouraging her fear. She's an adult. This is her decision.'' Dexter felt a little twinge, almost as if deep down, he didn't even believe the words.

''You know that's not true. You know it.'' Randy sat down and shook his head, his eyes sad. ''You need to encourage the people you love to do as much as they can, even if they're not necessarily making the safest choices. Your job is to help the one you love grow. You're holding Clem back by encouraging her fear. You're giving her every reason not to ride.''

''What am I supposed to do?'' Dexter asked. ''Put her on the horse? Make her ride if she doesn't want to? If she doesn't want to go, she doesn't have to go.''

''She won't go because she's frightened, not because she doesn't *want* to go. She *loved* being in those hills. You saw her face. You saw what she was like. Even when she was scared, she loved it."

Dexter was silent. Since her accident, he hadn't seen the smile that caused his heart to stop because of the sheer happiness in it.

"But..." Dexter's voice trailed off.

"I know her spill scared you just as much as it scared her. I know you were thinking about Joanna all over again. But Clem's all right. A couple of bruised ribs and a few stitches as a souvenir. But that's not all she's carrying around. She scared. And that's a life-changing burden."

"What if it happens again?" Dexter could barely get the words out. He stared at his friend. "I can't lose Clem."

"You can't live your life as if you're going to lose her," Randy said. "What are you going to do? Wrap her up in bubble wrap and hope that she doesn't get nicked? The only thing you can do is love her, man. And if you love her it means that you have to let her grow even if it's scary."

"Like you did with Joanna."

Randy wiped away a tear. He nodded. "Yes, like I did with Joanna. I wouldn't have changed a minute of what I had with her. I don't have regrets. I just miss her."

DEXTER FOUND CLEM in the stable brushing Archie later that evening.

"Sorry, it's been a while, boy," she was saying. "Soon we'll go for a trot around the property. You'll like that."

"I think he'd like going on the hunt for the other herd better," Dexter said.

Clem smiled at him. "You want to take him? He'd really appreciate the exercise."

He shook his head and crossed over toward her. "No."

Clem's eyebrows came together. "Then I don't know how he can join the hunt."

"If you ride him."

Clem laughed and brushed harder. "I thought we had this settled. You haven't been talking to Randy, have you?"

"I have been talking to Randy."

"And you set him straight, right?"

He was silent.

Clem stopped what she was doing and stared at Dexter. "You set him straight, didn't you?" she asked. For some reason her voice rose an octave.

He shook his head. "No, Clem. I think he finally set me straight."

"About what?"

"About you."

Clem sucked in air, making her ribs ache. ‘‘We’ve covered this. I’m not going.’’

‘‘And I need to tell you for the record that you should go. Randy’s right. If it’s the fear that’s stopping you, then that’s not acceptable.’’

That’s not acceptable.

Clem remembered those were the exact words she’d said to him when he’d told her he was retired.

‘‘Why are you making me do this?’’ she asked.

He shook his head, lifting a hand to her face. ‘‘I’m not making you do anything.’’ He ran a finger down her cheek. ‘‘You need to do this.’’

He dug around in his pocket, his movements awkward. ‘‘I have something for you.’’

‘‘I’m not going with you tomorrow,’’ she said stubbornly.

‘‘This doesn’t have anything to do with whether you’re going or not. It’s something I want you to have.’’

He held something that glittered.

‘‘My locket!’’ Clem exclaimed. ‘‘Where did you find it?’’

Dexter shook his head. ‘‘It’s not yours. But I want you to have it.’’

She was inexplicably touched. ‘‘You shouldn’t have bought me a new locket. It was just something my father gave me.’’

He was silent for a long time. Then he whispered, "I didn't buy this for you. It's Joanna's."

Clem stared at the locket. Joanna had died in a riding accident.

"Joanna loved life. She never let being afraid stop her from doing anything. She was so alive." Dexter's voice was so low she had to listen very carefully to catch all the words. "That's how I want you to be alive."

Clem shook her head. "I'm not brave like Joanna was. I'm not Joanna."

Dexter nodded. "I know you're not Joanna, but I think that you're every bit as brave. I think you have a form of courage that few people possess."

She felt tears spring to her eyes. "I haven't been through anything a thousand other people haven't already been through. And they probably recovered a lot quicker than I have."

"I'm not asking you to go, Clem. I want you to ask yourself the real reason you don't want to go." Dexter fastened the locket around her neck, his fingers lingering at the base of her skull. He gently rubbed the spot with the rough pad of his thumb.

"I can't. I can't change who I am." She didn't mean to sound so stubborn.

"Try."

She shook her head. "I won't. Not even for you.

I changed who I was for my ex-husband. I'm not going to do the same for you.''

He laughed shortly. ''Funny. I didn't think I was asking you to change. I just want you to accept who you really are. If you wanted to go to college, you would have done it years ago. If you wanted to move to Arizona, you'd have done it when your parents moved. If you wanted to work in an office where the only thing that you have to fear is a paper cut, you'd have found a job. No, Clem. I'm not asking you to change.''

She started brushing Archie again, in short, agitated strokes. ''Go away, Dexter.''

''Think about it, Clem.''

''Go away.''

He glanced at her, his eyes sad. ''Before, I said there was very little you could do that would disappoint me. I was wrong.'' Dexter walked out, leaving Clem to grapple with herself.

Later that night in bed, it occurred to her that that was the longest speech Dexter had ever made to her.

Clem wrestled with the competing thoughts. He was wrong. He *was* asking her to change. He was asking her to do something she didn't want to do.

Yes, she was frightened, but that didn't mean anything. Plenty of people never rode a horse, never even stepped inside a stable, and they went on to enjoy rich, fulfilling lives. She gasped as she realized she'd tried that already—when she'd married. That life had made her so lonely. Surrounded by all the people in suburbia, she'd never felt completely at ease. For years, she'd denied that she belonged on a horse. But even Nick, feckless as he was, had seen the truth and given her Archie.

She curled on to her side and clutched the locket.

Before, I said there was very little you could do that would disappoint me. I was wrong.

She tried to shut out Dexter's serious expression. He was asking too much. It wasn't as if she wasn't pulling her own weight. She worked on the books. She did laundry. She cooked. Every task a valuable contribution to the running of the ranch. She didn't need to be out in the thick of things.

You're bigger than that. Clem, there's only one life. And when it's done and over, will you be someone who played it safe and got nothing or someone who risked it all and got everything?

Now Clem had to try to shut off her mother's voice, as well. She'd spent her entire life listening to other voices. She just wanted to be left alone. She wanted to be left alone to make her own decisions. She sat up and turned on the light, taking off the locket. Joanna had worn this every day. It had been around her neck when she died.

With trembling fingers, Clem inserted her thumbnail into the small opening and gently twisted. She expected to see a picture of Joanna, but instead there were two pictures, one on each side. One of Dexter and one of Randy, trimmed so close that she could only see their eyes and their smiles. Clutching the locket in her hand, she turned off the light and waited for sleep.

The next morning, Clementine woke up with a terrible headache.

When she went down to breakfast, Dexter smiled at her, but she refused to return it. She saw the hurt on his face, but he still made a point of saying good-bye to her. The only thing she could think about was the fact she was a disappointment to him. He didn't need someone like her. He needed someone who had courage, who could take a spill and hop up ready to try again.

Clem threw herself into the laundry. But it seemed as if that chore got done a lot faster than she wanted. She cleaned the bathroom cabinets and the linen closet, as well. She worked furiously, hoping that the more she did, the less she would think about the fact that time was going by very slowly. When she finished she realized it wasn't even noon. Six hours before the guys would even be showing up for dinner.

She suppressed the urge to scream and pounded down the stairs and out the door. She was surprised to discover herself heading to the barn.

Archie nickered in greeting, looking inquisitively between her and the saddle.

Clem was tempted. She nuzzled her face against her horse's, he nipped at her ear. She combed her finger through his mane and remembered what it was like to ride him, feeling his taut muscles under her, the power and grace of his stride, the instant communication the two of them shared.

Dexter was right. When she was riding she did she feel as if her life was right. The only other time she'd felt that way was when she was kissing Dexter Scott. She suppressed a small smile, thinking back to that first impetuous kiss. How had she been so bold? She had kissed a complete stranger. She'd wanted to kiss him and she had. It didn't help her plight one iota, and she was still embarrassed by it, but she was glad she'd done it.

She stroked Archie's nose. "No, buddy. Not today. Tomorrow, maybe. Yes, definitely, tomorrow." With a quick kiss, she left him and crossed the few hundred yards to the bunkhouse, where Clem saw her mother walking toward her.

"Fancy meeting you here," Claire said.

Clem took the fresh linens from her mother's hands. "I finished early and I thought I'd save you the work. I'll do the bunkhouse."

Claire shook her head, her tongue clicking in the back of her throat. "It's not too much work. It's nice to be busy again. I thought you were doing the bathrooms.''

''Done.'' Clem tried to sound neutral, but knew she wasn't succeeding.

Her mother walked into the bunkhouse and blinked and then turned, her lips pursed with disapproval.

''What a mess,'' her mother sighed. ''I swear, men should never be left on their own.''

Clem surveyed the scene. It was messy, but nothing that couldn't be fixed with a stiff broom and some folding.

''Why don't you take a break? I'm feeling a little restless. I'll take care of it.''

Claire laughed. ''You won't see me turning down an offer like that! You just freed me up for a nap.'' She stared at her daughter. ''And when you finish this, what are you going to do?''

''There's some paperwork,'' Clem fudged.

Her mother's eyes were sharp. ''I thought you finished that up yesterday.''

''There're a couple of things I couldn't get settled.''

''Honey, you're twiddling your thumbs around here. You need to go with them,'' Claire said quietly. ''You need to be there.''

Clem swallowed. ''It's hard.''

''The best things in the world are hard. And

that's what makes you feel so good when you accomplish them, sweetie.'' Claire put a gentle hand on her daughter's face. ''You're up to the challenge.''

After her mother left, Clem walked quickly to the bathroom and gathered up the towels. Frijole, who was basking on top of a couple of them, yowled in protest.

''Sorry, girlie.'' Clem gathered up the cat, but Frijole was having none of it. She freed herself from Clem's grip with an indignant meow and stalked out of the bunkhouse. Clem continued to clean, finally opening up all the shades and the windows to let some air and light in. The ranch seemed empty without the noise of the men. She wasn't sure she liked having to wait until the end of the day to know what was happening.

You don't have to, echoed in her mind. *You could be right there.*

Clem took a broom from its place in the corner and cleared out the cobwebs from the ceiling. That task done, she started to strip the beds that had linens. As she pulled the pillowcases off one bed, she found something—a photograph.

She almost dropped the photo, the eyes shone at her so brightly. She sat on the lower bunk and held the picture in both hands. This had to be Joanna. The family resemblance to Dexter was far too strong for her to be anyone else. Clem's hand went to her throat as she saw the familiar locket hung around Joanna's neck.

You know what you need to do. Clem could almost feel Joanna talking to her. *You need to ride.*

Clem exhaled a long breath. Joanna was right.

"Thank you," she whispered.

Quickly, Clem changed the linen and placed the photo back under the pillow.

THAT EVENING WHEN CLEM reached the courtyard, the baritones of men's voices rose up to greet her. The courtyard had been transformed from an unloading dock to a party area. The trucks and trailers had been parked parallel to one another around the perimeter, and her father had rolled the large grill into the center under the lights. Latin music played in the background, piped in from the stereo in the living room. Claire had had the men set up a long picnic table and benches.

Even outside, her mother didn't forget decor. The tables were draped with bright white linen, and she'd put out the china along with cloth napkins and her best silverware. Clem smiled. It was always the same. Rather than using the traditional paper plates or tin for special occasions, Claire Wells always set the table with her mother's china. She never worried about any of it breaking. She knew the men who dined with her would be careful. After all, they made their living with their hands.

Clem could smell the tri-tip cooking on the grill, soaked in her mother's secret marinade and smiled as she walked closer. A chill had already descended, but the night was still beautiful. The men sat around the table, the delicate white porcelain in their hands being piled high with whatever they could get.

Clem's stomach growled. That was a relatively new sensation. She smiled, that was the cost of peace. Her mouth watered at the platters full of white and yellow corn and thick slabs of meat. Beans simmered in a large stainless steel pot set on one end of the enormous grill, and the bowls of coleslaw, chilled fruit salad and corn bread were rapidly emptying. Several coolers were filled to the brim with ice, chilling sodas and Mexican beer.

Her father was right in the heart of things, flipping the tri-tip with a long pair of barbecue tongs. He loved these parties, and presided over them with the jolly demeanor of Santa Claus, encouraging his guests to eat more. Her mother sat at the end of the table engaged in an intense conversation with one of the hired hands as she waited for her turn at the buffet.

"Get a plate, Clem," her father called.

Clem got herself a plate, noticing that Randy had

two plates. There was no doubt that he'd be going back for seconds or maybe even thirds.

"You'd better shake that pretty tail. The corn bread's almost gone," a voice whispered in her ear.

She swung around to see Dexter Scott's moss-green eyes. They burned with the same smoky look he'd had days before.

"Don't you make any noise at all?" she asked, using irritation to mask the butterflies that started fluttering in her stomach. "You scared the death out of me."

She tried to put some coleslaw on to her plate, frustrated because she saw her hand trembling. How could he do that to her?

"Here, let me," he said. He shifted his own full plate to his forearm, took hers, and then with his free hand heaped it with coleslaw.

"You do that well."

"I do a lot of things well." Dexter shrugged, as if it was no big deal, but the sparkle in his eyes belied his modesty.

Clem couldn't quell the twinge of excitement. The butterflies had managed to migrate to her chest and throat. Even after the way she'd treated him, Dexter Scott was flirting with her.

"Did you guys have a successful day?" she asked.

He nodded. "Ryan found them, Clem, and they're prettier than the last bunch."

"Are they easy to get to?"

He nodded. "Easy enough if it doesn't rain."

She shook her head. "You might be out of luck. I heard a system was coming in late tonight."

He tightened his lips. "That would be bad. They're farther down the creek bed. It's already up to their knees."

"It probably won't rise until the second day of rain."

He handed her her plate. "Let's pray for small favors."

She took her plate and then whispered, "I'm sorry about this morning."

"This morning?" he asked, his tone neutral.

"I was rude to you."

"I didn't notice." Dexter searched the corn for a plump ear for her. He put it on her plate.

"That's very nice of you not to notice. But I was angry and I was rude. I didn't really want to listen to what you had to say."

Dexter held up a piece of tri-tip and she held out her plate.

"Clem. I shouldn't have said I'd be disappointed in you. I wouldn't be. I like you just the way you are. Whatever you decide."

Even though the words came out of his mouth,

Clem noticed he didn't meet her eyes. They walked to the picnic table and she realized with a twinge of disappointment that he had no intention of sitting next to her. In fact, he moved to sit next to her mother.

"So what are you planning to do tomorrow?" Clem asked, forcing her voice to be casual. She addressed the whole table, but she kept her eyes on Dexter.

"We're going to try to beat the rain and bring the last of the suckers in," answered Ryan, who was on her left.

"Yeah, if all goes well, we might make it home for Thanksgiving." Across from her, Randy nodded. "We'll be out of your hair quick enough."

Clem winced at his tone. She hated the fact that Randy, jovial Randy, had become so distant. She swallowed. He'd been right about her—and had been brave enough, and kind enough, to say so. And she'd ignored him.

"You're not in our hair at all," Claire protested. "In fact, since Thanksgiving is just next week, I was planning to invite you to stay for dinner. You deserve some relaxation."

"Yes," Clem agreed. She tried to meet Randy's eyes. "We appreciate all you've done for us. For me."

Randy gave her a polite smile.

"So what time were you planning to go out in the morning?"

"Early," groaned her father who had just come to join them. Clem scooted closer to Ryan to make room for him. "And I for one can't wait for this to be over. My butt is so sore that Claire has had to rub liniment into it." He winked at her. "Not that the rubbing's a bad thing."

"Dad." Clem rolled her eyes. "So do you need any extra help?"

"No," Ryan dismissed her concern with a confident shake of his head. "I don't think that you'll have to track down any extra guys for us. The ones we've been working with have been working out just great. With your dad, I think we have enough."

"I wasn't thinking about a lot of extra help. Just me."

CHAPTER TWELVE

WHEN CLEM WOKE UP the next morning, she saw the predicted thunderstorms had arrived. Torrents of rain prevented her from even seeing the courtyard from her window. She grimaced as she dressed. She'd certainly picked good weather to make her comeback. She brightened. Maybe they'd call it off today and she'd be given a reprieve.

When she walked into the kitchen Randy greeted her with a big hug, careful not to squeeze too hard. "Welcome back, Clem."

She gave him a little shaky smile. "It's raining pretty hard out there."

Dexter walked into the dining room, covered head to toe with his rain gear. He shook off the excess water.

His eyes lit up when he saw Clem. "The rain looks bad," Dexter said, his eyes sweeping over her face. "Maybe we should put this off a couple of days."

Ryan shook his head. "Not a good idea. If we don't do something, the cows'll get caught in that gorge. We have a little window now, and I think that we should just take it.''

''A little rain won't hurt us,'' Jim announced when he walked into the kitchen. He poured himself a cup of coffee, then looked at his daughter. ''Clem, you'd better put on another layer.''

''We'd better get going if we're going to get the cattle out before the creek rises,'' Dexter said to everyone.

Clem drank down her orange juice and started to follow the men outside, when her father pulled her aside.

''How are those ribs?''

''Feeling better,'' Clem said.

''You sure you want to do this? No one's going to think any less of you. You've done a heck of a good job.''

Clem looked up at her father. She wasn't sure she wanted to do it. The smart thing was probably to go upstairs and get back into bed.

''I'm really scared, Dad,'' she admitted.

Jim Wells nodded. ''I understand. I'm scared too.''

''You are?''

''Sure. Believe me, both Dexter and I would feel a lot more comfortable if we knew you were cooking instead of riding.''

She would, too.

''But, this isn't about what we want. It's about what you want. Now, let's go and do good out there.''

Clem smiled. ''Thanks, Dad.''

''So what do you want to do?'' Randy addressed Dexter. ''We have the rest of the cattle penned up past that ridge. They'll need to come through the creek, then veer up along the gorge path if we want to get them to the field. The rain makes this more dangerous.''

Dexter looked at Ryan, who shrugged.

''Personally, I'd rather be in front of a warm fire,'' Ryan put in. ''But I'm so anxious to finish, I can taste it. It is steep.''

''It's suicide.'' That was all Clem had to say. What they were talking about was crazy. If it worked, the job would be done in a matter of hours. If it didn't, the best case scenario was that they'd end up working through Thanksgiving all the way to Christmas and then some. Worst case scenario the path would erode under the pressure of the herd, sending both cattle and rider plunging into the gorge.

''Only if we don't get through in time,'' Dexter reminded her.

''Don't forget about slides,'' Jim Wells said.

''Slides?'' Dexter looked at Jim.

The older man nodded. ''You need to be careful about mud slides. Once this slate gets soaked, the whole side of the mountain might come down on you.''

''How long do you think we have?'' Randy asked.

''A day,'' Jim estimated. ''If it continues, we'll be benched until this storm's over. Then another week until things dry out.''

''I wouldn't mind that. Then you'd definitely be here for Thanksgiving,'' Clem offered brightly.

They ignored her.

''Who knows where those cows will be next week,'' Ryan said thoughtfully. ''They're certainly not going to be waiting for us to come back. Right now we've got them holed up, and they aren't going anywhere until this rain passes.''

''It's up to you, boss,'' Randy looked at Dexter.

''No. It's up to Clem.'' Dexter said quietly.

Clem shook her head. ''Nope. I'm not making decisions like these. You guys know what you can do.''

''This is your call. Do you think we can do it?'' Dexter asked.

''The horses are fresh. How fresh are you?'' Clem looked around. ''I know I'm fresh. I've had nearly three weeks' rest.''

Ryan grinned. ‘‘Fresh enough. Got a whole six hours of sleep last night.’’

Clem hesitated.

‘‘Come on, Clem. You can do it,’’ Randy encouraged her.

She really wanted to go home. She wanted to be dry. She wanted to be safe. She swallowed hard, and a few seconds felt like hours passing. They were waiting for her to make a decision, but there was no judgment in their eyes, only friendship. She sighed heavily. ‘‘Let’s stop talking and get going.’’

‘‘Clem?’’ Her father asked. ‘‘Are you sure?’’

Clem nodded. ‘‘Let’s do it.’’

Clem expected her words to send terror coursing through her; instead there was only a little twinge. As she rode Archie across the wide pasture, up the muddy trail where the cows were, she realized that instead of fear, she was feeling anticipation. Her heart was thumping not because she was terrified, but because she was excited.

Why?

I’m not asking you to go, Clem. I want you to ask yourself the real reason you don’t want to go.... I just want you to accept who you really are.

Dexter’s words came back to her. And she grinned in realization. Who would have thought a retired cowboy would have been able to give her herself?

"Quit daydreaming, Clem. We've got work to do!" Randy hollered.

Clem looked up to see that Dexter had dropped back to trot with her.

"How you doing?" Dexter asked.

She nodded, wanting to shout, wanting to stop and hug him. She'd found herself for the first time in thirty-two years and she had him to thank for that.

"Fine," she said.

He searched her face. "You look strong," he commented.

"I am strong," Clementine stated. His smile reached his eyes. He tipped his hat to her, some water running in front of his face. "Good luck today. We'll talk later," he promised.

Then he rode to catch up with Randy.

Clem couldn't wait. After this was over, after all the cows were accounted for, she and Dexter would need to take a ride somewhere in his truck and talk and talk and talk. But now was the time for work.

When they reached the glen there was a little break in the weather, and Clem beheld the most beautiful sight she'd ever seen—the last two hundred cows. Even after Dex and the Millers had arrived, she hadn't allowed herself to completely believe there'd be an end to this fiasco. But there the cows were, and here she was. She shook her head, truly appreciating the hard work that these men had accomplished over the past weeks.

"Careful, these are a little more jittery than the last," Dexter warned, when she brought Archie up close to Calisto.

Clem laughed. "More jittery?" She couldn't imagine.

"If we get them from behind, we can turn them along the channel."

Ryan indicated the desired route with his fingers. "Once through that, there's only one way to go and that's right into a corral at the bottom."

It seemed too easy to Clem. "Unless the path gives way. This rain isn't going to let up more than this, is it?"

They all looked up at the clouds, which darkened and rolled as she spoke.

Jim agreed with her. "If the path goes, we'll end up with more than a few stuck cows."

"It's a tight one," Ryan said, his head angled toward the herd. "If ever we have a chance to do this, it's now."

Clem sucked in her breath. "So it's now."

She glanced at Dexter, who was studying the terrain below them. Finally he looked at her, water dripping off the back of his hat. He flashed her an encouraging smile.

He turned to Jim. "You and Ryan take the back.

We'll take the side. When you're ready, drive the cows our way. We'll take our cue from you."

"Just be sure to stay away from the wall. Once they get going, we have to stay behind or they'll run right over us."

"Okay. Let's do it."

Her heart pounded in her chest, and Clem didn't even feel the ache in her ribs or the cold on her face, but she did feel a little fear. Just a little.

Dexter urged Calisto right next to her. "You don't have to do this," he said, his voice low, his eyes scanning her face.

"Are you telling me you don't want me to do this?" she asked. If he said, yes, she would leave in a heartbeat. "If you say so, I'll go home right now. Honest. I will."

His face was torn. "Don't ask me that."

"Just say, 'Clem, I think you're still a little bruised. Why don't you sit this out?'" she encouraged him. "Then I'll just turn around and go home."

Dexter was silent. "It's very dangerous."

She fiddled with Joanna's locket. "Are you telling me to go home?"

Dexter's eyes were trained on her hand, on the locket. After a long moment, he shook his head and said clearly, "No."

She swallowed hard, her heart hurting because

she knew exactly what that single word had cost him to say. Even though he wouldn't forgive himself for Joanna, he still was willing to take a risk for her. She felt her resolve strengthen. If he had that much faith in her, then she should have it in herself.

"Clem."

"Yes?"

"I just want you to know that I'll do everything I can to keep you safe."

She touched his cheek. "You already have."

His green eyes flickered over her face, and his mouth settled into a vulnerable line. "Okay, let's go get them."

She nodded. "Let's go get them."

The fifteen minutes it took for them to get into position seemed like an eternity. Dexter deliberately kept his distance, probably as much for her peace of mind as his. He directed her to her spot with a wave of his hand. In position, Jim and Ryan started the herd, and as hoped, the cattle began to herd in the right direction.

It was invigorating.

The feel of Archie beneath her, the whipping of the rain across her face gave her an adrenaline rush that she'd never allowed herself to enjoy before. There was no way in the world that she could ever feel this way if she was stuck in the kitchen. There was nothing wrong with cooking, but this was better.

In this imperfect setting, she'd found peace. She had a place, a purpose. Here, action was ten times more valued than thinking. She'd spent too much of her time thinking, too much time being afraid. Now was the time for *doing*.

And suddenly, the kiss she'd planted on Dexter the morning she'd found him was no longer a source of embarrassment. She laughed out loud. It was the symbol of a woman who was acting on who she was. From now on, she needed to do what she wanted. She needed to go out on her own, without the safety net provided by her parents, by Dexter.

She needed to depend on herself.

DEXTER SHOULD HAVE BEEN thinking about the job, but he was absorbed by the beauty and the joy on Clem's face. She was drenched, but her face was flushed with excitement. He felt a deep twinge. That was exactly how Joanna had looked when she was riding. That was exactly the expression she always had in her eyes.

"She's beautiful, isn't she?" Randy asked from beside him.

Dexter looked at his friend sideways and agreed. "Yes, she is. But she's not like Joanna."

Randy gave him a half smile. "No, she's not. She's very different."

"Joanna would have liked Clem."

Randy smiled. "I think they would have been the best of friends."

"You think Joanna was happy?"

Randy nodded. "I *know* she was."

Archie had begun to prance in place as they waited for the cattle to reach them, and Clem laughed in delight.

"My God," he whispered. "It's as wrong to try to suppress that spirit as it is to hobble a horse."

Randy nodded. "She was meant to be out here. Just like Joanna was."

"Clem wanted me to stop her. She wanted me to tell her to go home."

"Aren't you glad you didn't?" Randy smiled. "That's why I've always mourned Joanna, but never regretted anything, not one thing."

Dexter finally understood, and he felt the weight of his guilt lift from his shoulders. Before he could thank his friend, Clem let out a whoop. The cattle were coming.

The clamor was deafening, and pounding hooves shook the ground. Dexter forgot about Clem as he watched to see which way the cattle were heading. The cows seemed complacent. They'd been holed up in the rain, and all they wanted to do was get to a dry place.

Dexter sighed in relief. They would be done inside two hours. They would be wet and cold, but the bulk of the work would be done. No doubt, there would still be some strays to find, but he knew the area was pretty much cleared.

He watched a smiling Clem handle her part of the line with expertise. Her father was shouting something at her and she waved and nodded. Then she shot a glance in his direction and her smile widened. Dexter had to look away the smile was so bright.

Over the next hour, Dexter knew what he had to do. Tonight after they'd cleaned up and celebrated, he'd drive her to town. They had so much to say to each other, so many things to plan. They'd find a small, dark restaurant and talk. Really talk. About the stuff that women liked to talk about. Feelings. Love. He could do that.

"Careful!" Ryan's shout of warning made Dexter look up.

The cows were getting a little out on line of Jim's side, but the older man soon got them organized again. Dexter tried to find Clem in the clamor, but the rain obscured his view.

There were two more shouts, and then he heard Clem swearing and relief flooded through him.

As they all advanced to the point at which the path narrowed, he saw that Clem was close to the mountain slope. He stood up on Calisto, silently urging her to be careful about getting pinned. When he couldn't see her, his heart thudded in his throat. He released the breath he hadn't known he'd held when Archie could suddenly be seen behind a tree with Clementine safely on board. She was fine. Today was going to be a good day.

A loud expletive had Dexter starting to search. Who was in trouble? Then he saw Jim Wells was being squeezed toward the bank of the creek by the cows. He was at the narrowest point of the paths, where the cows had to be slowed to single file. Dexter spurred his horse to see what he could do. Before he could get there, Clem and Archie appeared. She'd doubled back when she'd heard her father's yell. Somehow, she managed to slow the cattle, so Jim could shoot through. Dexter, who was on the other side of the herd, could only watch.

Behind her the cows were coming up fast, and she and Archie were caught in the flow.

DEXTER SAW A SMALL OPENING. If he could drive the cows toward the side, Clem might have a chance to get through. He didn't dare think about what would happen if he failed. And he definitely wouldn't think about the fact that if he'd told her to go home, she would have turned around and gone. He raced toward the last place he'd seen Clem, but went cold when he heard Archie scream. Frantic, he searched for Clem. Nowhere. It was as if she'd disappeared off the face of the earth.

As the last of the cows surged forward, he saw Jim Wells riding toward him, his face drawn and pale.

"Where is she?" His voice was ragged, and he never stopped looking for his daughter.

Dexter didn't say anything, just spurred Calisto toward the creek bank. Jim Wells was right behind him.

It was eerie how quiet it had become. The rain had calmed to a drizzle and the sound of hoofbeats dimmed as the herd moved away. Dex saw the trampled body of one of the dogs and stopped cold. He didn't want to look any further. He couldn't look. It was the same thing that had happened with Joanna.

"I think she disappeared around here." Clem's father pointed as he dismounted, slipping in the mud. "I can't see anything. Damn it, Scott. Help me find her. She needs our help. She could be dead."

"No!" Dexter denied, his voice fierce with his feelings as he bolted off Calisto. "Clem is *not* dead. She's stronger than that." The anguish in the older

man's voice broke through the hold that had held Dexter frozen.

Randy and Ryan came racing over.

"Who went down?" Randy asked.

"Clem!" Dexter shouted. "She went down around here."

Randy and Ryan were off their horses in a split second, the four of them searching through the deep brush and mud for Clementine.

"Oh, God. There she is," Dexter yelled, and was sliding down the ravine, mud smearing the back of his slicker. "Randy, she's right over there, by you!"

It seemed as if it took an eternity for Dexter to make his way to Clem. He prayed the entire time.

"She's still alive. She's breathing!" Randy yelled.

She was breathing. Clem was breathing.

"Ryan, call 911," Randy ordered. He was gently feeling Clem's limbs.

Ryan was already talking rapidly into his cell phone.

"Clem, can you hear me?" Dexter talked softly in her ear, as he grasped her hand.

Clem didn't respond.

"Clem, hold on." Jim was beside him. "Don't worry. They've got a great hospital. They'll send in a helicopter. She'll be at the hospital in no time."

"They want to talk to you, Jim. You know best how to direct them here." Ryan handed the phone to the older man, who walked away a few steps and began to talk with great authority. Dexter felt a small squeeze on his hand. Clem was staring up at him.

"Hey, Clem," Dexter greeted her. "I think you were trying to take the herd on all by yourself."

She gave a weak smile.

"Did you think you could fly?" he asked.

"D-Dad?" It took every ounce of energy for her to gasp out the word.

"He's fine," Dexter said, brushing her hair back from her face. The scar from her last fall was still livid. "He's right here, giving directions to everyone."

She nodded and closed her eyes.

A long minute crept by and her eyes opened again.

"Ar-Archie?"

Dexter looked up. He hadn't even thought about Archie.

Ryan leaned over, his face sad. "Sorry, Clem. He didn't make it."

Clem closed her eyes. Tears leaked out the sides.

"Y-you w-were r-right." She tried to lift her hand from his.

He held on tighter, thinking she could take warmth from him. ''About what?'

''D-dangerous.'' She tried to laugh and wheezed instead. ''Am I okay?''

''Your dad's making arrangements to get you out of here. You'll be fine. Anything feel broken?''

''Everything feels broken.'' Clem attempted another smile, then passed out.

Jim clicked off the phone and noticed her closed eyes. ''Is she...''

Dexter shook his head. ''No, she's still breathing.''

''They said to keep her still. They're on their way and they have this number if they can't find us.''

The twenty minutes it took for the helicopter to arrive seemed to take an eternity. Dexter sat next to Clem and waited with Jim. Randy and Ryan went ahead to tell Claire. It was something that needed to be done in person.

''She saved me,'' Jim said, his voice caught in his throat. ''If Clem hadn't been there, I'd be the one in the ditch. And if you hadn't diverted the herd, she'd have taken more than a little tumble.''

''I didn't do anything special.''

''How did you get to her so fast?''

''Panic.'' Dexter couldn't smile. He moved closer to Clem when she moaned.

''I did this to her,'' Dexter said finally.

Jim Wells looked at him sharply. ''You weren't even close.''

''Earlier, she asked me if I thought she should go. She told me that if I said no, she'd turn around and go back home. I should have said no.''

''And she would have never ranched again,'' Jim said. ''I saw how scared she was. I think you gave her a gift, Scott. You gave her the right to make her own decisions.''

If only Dexter could believe that. Instead he said roughly, ''Where the hell are they?''

''They'll be here.''

Jim put a gentle hand on Clem's forehead. ''I'm going to wait in the clearing for them.''

Dexter nodded. He watched Clem's shallow breathing. ''You're a damn good cowboy,'' he said with a whisper.

He didn't expect her to answer back, but kept talking to her. ''I meant it as a compliment. Honest.'' His voice broke. ''I'm sorry about this, Clem. I should've told you to go home.'' His throat closed and he felt tears gather in his throat. He blinked in surprise.

Was it his imagination or did Clem squeeze his hand?

Her eyes were open again. ''Y-you're n-not crying, are you?'' she wheezed.

He touched her face. ''Clem, I love you.''

''C-cowboys d-don't cry,'' she told him, her own eyes filling with tears.

''This one does.'' He brought her hand to his face so she could feel the tears for Joanna, for her, for himself, flooding out of him.

She shook her head and gave him a weak smile. ''S-sorry. D-don't have a hankie.'' Tears slipped down the side of her face.

Dexter laughed, then he ordered her, ''Don't die on me, Clem.''

She rolled her eyes. ''D-don't intend to die. T-too much living t-to do.''

The roar of the helicopter interrupted her. Dexter leaned over her to protect her from the dust that was being kicked up.

''L-loud,'' Clem said.

''They're here. You'll be fixed up good as new.''

In a flurry of efficient motion, the emergency medical technicians took over, waving Dexter out of the way. Once they'd strapped her onto the gurney, Dexter was filled with an overwhelming sense of surrender. Is that what love did? Made one surrender? Or was it in surrendering one gained the most strength?

''One of you can go with her,'' the pilot shouted over the roar of the helicopter blades.

Jim pointed to Dex. ''You go. I'll be right behind you.''

"You'll be fine?" Dexter looked toward the horses.

Wells gave a ghost of a smile. "I'll be better when I know she's okay."

With a nod, Dexter climbed into the chopper.

CHAPTER THIRTEEN

CLEM PROPPED HER LEG on the stool her mother put out for her. Frijole sat in her lap, rubbing her head against Clem's cast. When she tired of that she used her claws, slowly shaving away the plaster. Six weeks had come and gone since the accident. Clem had spent Thanksgiving in the hospital eating bland turkey and complaining about the itching in her cast. She'd suffered a broken leg, arm and collar-bone, along with a nasty concussion. She'd been in and out of consciousness for nearly six days and had had surgery to put steel pins in both her arm and her leg. Dexter had become a permanent fixture in the hospital, sleeping in a chair by her bed for much of her stay. Even though they spent a lot of time together, they never discussed the accident.

They'd talked about the weather and how Randy and Ryan were doing. They even talked a little about Archie. Clem had mourned her beloved friend, staring out of the hospital window, not really believing he was gone. She'd been sent home in early December, and the first time she'd visited the stable and seen he wasn't there, she'd cried. Archie had been the only constant in her life for the past six years.

Not long after she arrived home, Randy and Ryan began to make preparations to leave. It was amazing to Clem that in such a short space of time, they'd managed to become like brothers to her. In the end, her feral cows had made a hefty profit for both the Millers and the ranch. On the day they'd hitched up their trailers and loaded up their horses and dogs, Clem had finally been able to stand up on crutches to say goodbye.

Randy had given her a big bear hug, then patted the cast on her leg. "I hope this doesn't put you off cowboying."

She had smiled and shaken her head. "Nope. They'll slow me down, but as soon as they come off, I'll be back on the horse."

"Then you might need this." He had stuffed something into her pocket.

"What is it?"

"Think of it as a Christmas gift from the Miller brothers."

Clem realized it was a check that amounted to their share of the cows. "No!" Clem had protested. "This is your money. You earned it and some."

"I told you we were only in it for the thrill.

You'll need to buy a new horse. This might get you started."

Clem had kissed him soundly. "I'm going to miss you."

"I'm going to miss you, too, Sleeping Beauty."

Ryan had hugged her next.

"You've been the voice of sanity," Clem had whispered. "I don't know why some girl hasn't snatched you up yet."

Ryan had grinned. "Haven't found one that can run fast enough yet."

"Will we see you around?" Randy had asked, his head poking out of the passenger side of the truck window.

She'd nodded. "You'll see me around."

Clem had stared at the empty courtyard. It was the end of an adventure.

Dexter had stayed through the Christmas holidays. Now that she was recovering, she kept waiting for the "big talk," a time when they would sort through their feelings and decide what step they wanted to take next. But it never came. Over the past six weeks, they had talked about horses, about her injuries, about her plans. But they hadn't talked about their future. Every morning she woke up, expecting that this would be the day he'd tell her he was moving on or at least moving back to Barstow.

But every morning, he just ate breakfast with her before starting to work with New Horse.

He spent hours with New Horse.

She didn't remember much about the accident, but she did remember him saying he loved her. Or at least, she thought she did. But as the days turned into weeks, she began to attribute his words to panic more than anything else. It was a reasonable conclusion. He'd thought she was going to die. People often said things in times of crisis that they didn't mean or, at least, didn't want to be held to.

Her father came and sat next to her. He gave Frijole a scratch behind the ear.

"I guess it's too late for a new herd?" Jim Wells asked.

"You're going back to retirement, remember?" Clem reminded him. She inhaled the crisp January sunshine. There was a wonderful smell to it, as if spring was just around the corner. "Two weeks and these puppies come off. A couple of weeks of physical therapy and I'm back to normal. But I don't think that even then I'll be in any shape for dealing with my own herd of cattle, not even Herefords."

"Well, you'll want to be planning for next season."

Clem shook her head and said seriously, "There's not going to be a next season. Not with me at the helm, anyway. I've been thinking about what I'm going to do in the future. Dad, I'm not going to ranch anymore."

"What do you mean?"

"I mean I don't want the ranch. I don't want to put out a herd."

"Then what are you going to do?"

Clem was silent for a long time.

"You're always welcome to join your mother and me in Arizona."

She smiled gently and grabbed his hand and squeezed.

"No. I've been thinking about going out on my own. After I pay you back, I'm going to invest in a couple of good horses and see where I end up. I'm going to work some odd cowboy jobs, maybe on a dude ranch or something. I need to spend some time alone."

"Honey, are you sure it's safe?" Jim Wells looked concerned.

Clem laughed. "I don't know if it's safe, but right now I just want to see where I end up."

"But what about your Dexter?"

Your Dexter. The words hurt more than her ribs. She gave a small laugh. "I don't think he's *my* Dexter, Dad."

"He seems to think he is."

"He's got a funny way of showing it." Clem's voice was clipped.

"Maybe he's just waiting until the right moment."

Clem wondered. "Well, he better hurry up, because I'm a busy woman. I've got people to meet, places to go."

"Speaking of going." Her father picked up her hand. "I came out to tell you we're going back to Arizona the weekend after you get your cast off. We'll wait until you can make it up and down the stairs all right. Your mother thinks it's time we got back to our life."

Clem smiled. "And you? What are you missing?"

Her father smiled, his eyes nostalgic. "Riding with those boys made me realize that I have it pretty good. A lovely wife, a smart daughter, enough money to be comfortable. I think I'm just going to enjoy myself. If you're serious about not wanting the ranch, we may just put it up for sale."

Clem felt her throat tighten. "I'm going to miss you, Dad."

"You can always work on a dude ranch in Arizona."

"Maybe I will. Maybe I will."

TOO QUICKLY HER PARENTS were getting ready to leave. Clem couldn't stop the tears from forming.

"You'll call when you get there?"

Her mother nodded. "Of course. And I'll talk to you Sunday."

Standing on two good legs, she hugged her mother with two good arms. "Thank you. Thank you for everything."

"Now, you be nice to Dexter. He's a good man."

Clem gave her a watery smile. "He is a good man, even if he doesn't talk that much."

"He will, sweetheart. He will," her mother assured her.

Her father gave her a resounding bear hug.

"Don't like goodbyes. We're going to see you at Easter, right?"

Clem nodded. "I'm coming down at Easter."

"You might like it in Arizona," her father said with a wink.

"I might."

She stood and waved until their car was out of sight. Her shoulders slumped as she realized how deserted the place was. Dexter was almost invisible the way that he moved around. Soon he would tell her it was time for him to go and she would be left alone with Frijole and Cowchip.

"I guess it's just us," a voice said behind her.

Clem jumped.

Dexter was sitting on the porch, his gray felt hat pulled down over his eyes, Frijole in his lap, yet another victim of those hands of his. The only part of his face she could see was his mouth. He was smiling.

"Are you up for a ride?" he invited. "It's early."

She frowned. She'd only had the cast off her leg for three days. But the doctor hadn't said anything about not riding, and she'd be riding an older horse, so it probably wouldn't put a lot of strain on her leg.

She looked up and nodded. *This is where he tells me that he's leaving, too.* She walked to the stable and Dexter walked alongside her. She didn't know which horse to ride. For so long there had only been Archie.

"Why don't you take New Horse?" Dexter suggested as he pulled the horse out of his stall, already saddled.

Clem hesitated. "I'm not sure I should. He's pretty wild, right?"

"Was," Dexter corrected her. "I've been working out most of his kinks. Here, I'll give you a boost. I know he's not Archie, but he needs someone like you."

Clem let him help her onto New Horse. He skittered a little but quickly settled down. Clem rode him around the courtyard a couple of times and liked his responsiveness. She patted his mane. "You are a sweetie," she crooned.

Dexter joined her on Calisto.

"Where to?" Dexter asked.

"Let's just go around the property," Clem said. "I haven't seen it since before Thanksgiving."

They rode in silence.

Finally, Dexter broke it. "You still have about two dozen of those cows hiding up in the mountains."

Clem grinned. "That will be the next rancher's problem, won't it?"

"You giving up ranching?" His voice was sober.

Clem nodded. "Yes. I thought I'd go out on the road. Work as a hand at other ranches."

Dexter was silent.

They rode for a while when he said suddenly, "You'd make a good one."

"What?" Clem asked.

"A good hand. You'd make a good hand."

"Oh." Clem smiled. "Thanks. It's a big compliment coming from you."

"If you want a recommendation or something, I'd be happy to give you one."

"Okay, thanks." Clem closed her eyes and took in a deep breath. She wanted his declaration of undying love and he was offering her a letter of recommendation. Only Dexter Scott would be that obtuse.

DEXTER SAT NEXT TO CLEM knowing he was running out of time. He'd heard her talk about wanting to work other ranches. Randy had thought it was a positive step. That he should let her get it out of her system. It was a way for her to gain some independence and self-respect. Randy had been right about most everything, so Dexter was very careful to not mention anything about loving her or needing her or wanting to marry her. And she didn't say anything about loving him or needing him or wanting to marry him, either. She looked different to him now. She looked content.

He asked, his voice casual, "What's your first move?"

He stared at her, aching to pull her close, but not daring.

"I found some ads in *Western Horseman.* I'm going to follow up on some of them."

"What are you going to do with Frijole and Cowchip?" He sounded as if he was making casual conversation, but he really wanted her to tell him what she planned to do after she'd worked on other people's ranches.

Clem shook her head. "I haven't actually thought that far ahead. I just thought I'd take them with me."

"I'll take them if you like," he offered. "I have

a few mice Frijole'd find tasty. Lots of room for Cowchip to hang around."

"Thanks. I'll think about it."

There was nothing else to say until they rode up to a gate.

"I've got it," Dexter said. He slid off Calisto and worked the lock. She caught Calisto's reins and walked the horse through while Dex closed the gate behind them.

Dexter felt the gates in his heart open. She'd been the one to show him that his heart still worked and a heart that beat was a heart that could love.

There was another long silence between them. It seemed to punctuate their relationship.

Dexter looked around the beautiful mountain property. Clem had been the one to show him that he was wasting his life behind the gates he'd built. It was time for him to learn to live out in the open, just as it was time for her to be on her own. "I guess there's not much more for me here."

She nodded. "I suppose it's time for you to be moving on."

He looked up at the sky that was just starting to clear. His stomach knotted, but he forced his voice to be light. "Any idea where you're going first?"

"I faxed one place my résumé, and they want to see me."

"Where?"

"Nevada."

Nevada wasn't so far away. She could find her way back to him.

"So what are *you* planning to do?" Clem asked suddenly. "Are you still retired?"

"Call it semiretired," Dexter amended. "The old Victorian needs quite a bit of attention. And Randy said he'd call if there was a job that was particularly exciting."

Clem nodded, but didn't comment.

"I might plant some grass." He couldn't look at her. "Kids like to play on grass."

"Yes, they do," Clem agreed.

They rode for another twenty minutes until the ranch house came into sight. He turned to her and said, "You'll need a good horse."

"My dad will let me take whichever one I want. And thanks to Randy and Ryan, I've got enough money to buy a new one."

Dexter gave a short laugh. "No offense, but you're not going to get very far with any of your dad's horses, and a new one is going to take some getting used to."

Clem's face dimmed. He could tell how much she still felt the loss of her horse.

"Think you could handle New Horse?" he asked before she could get too sad.

DEXTER WASN'T LOOKING directly at Clem so she had a hard time figuring out exactly what he was asking. "Probably."

"He's still a little skittish, but in a little time, he'll be a good horse," Dexter said. "I've seen you ride. You're good. If you used one of your dad's as your main horse and worked with New Horse every day, it wouldn't take long for you to be a great team. Shoot, you could even rename him. You'd be taken more seriously showing up with New Horse than with any stock your father has."

"I would," Clem said slowly. "But I know he's expensive. I don't think I can afford it."

"I'm not selling New Horse. I'm giving him to you."

Clem's throat closed. "Why?"

Dexter answered her question with a question. "Do you want him?"

"Uh..."

"Do you want him?" he repeated.

"Yes!" The word burst out of her. "Thank you."

"You follow that dream of yours. But do me one favor?"

Clem was mesmerized by his gaze. Wordless, she nodded.

"While you're following your head, make sure you listen to your heart, too."

She nodded.

"Farewell, friend." As if he couldn't help himself, he caught her to him and hugged her tightly. "I hope you find what you're looking for."

CHAPTER FOURTEEN

Somewhere northeast of Barstow, California

SPITTING DUST. If there was anything that Dexter Scott hated worse than spitting dust, it was scraping paint from a monster of a house that had been left far too long without care. He brushed the sweat off his forehead with the sleeve of his flannel shirt. It was a sunny April day, but there was still plenty of desert chill in the air. He looked up at the house. He'd finished much of the interior, opened up the little alcove. Dexter realized how odd it was that something terrible could sometimes be a blessing.

Clem's accident was terrible, but it was a blessing. It had made him realize that if one didn't snatch love when one had the chance, it was gone. He didn't know where Clem was, but he had a feeling she was close. He'd made it his business to know at least the general area she was in. She'd started in Nevada, then moved on to Texas for a few months.

She dropped him an occasional postcard, but he hadn't heard from her in nearly two months. He knew she was right to go. And he knew he was right to let her.

He'd realized he had his own life to straighten out. His house needed fixing and the yard needed work. He looked at the brown grass. He'd ordered some grass plugs and had put down some compost already. He'd tackled the overgrown rosebush, pruning it back to a reasonable size. He'd also got rid of all the debris littering the property. He knew exactly why he was fixing up the place. He was still hoping Clem would come looking for him. Then they could start over.

A little bit at a time.

And if Clem didn't come back, he'd go out and track her down. Not to run her life or anything, but to ask whether she'd mind if he rode shotgun with her.

Calisto whinnied, and Dexter looked over his shoulder because he knew the horse wasn't whinnying at him. A truck rumbled down the road, tires crunching the red desert sand.

His heart jumped to his throat.

Dexter climbed down off the ladder and shook paint chips out of his hat. Then he walked toward the truck as it pulled slowly to a stop. A trailer was hitched to the back, and a dog—Cowchip—barked from the passenger seat. Dex was sure that Frijole was in a cage, very unhappy.

After what seemed like an eternity, Clem opened the door and stepped out. She was wearing a pair of faded blue jeans and a blue chambray shirt. Her head was bare, and her hair fell around her face in soft waves. She looked straight at him and walked over to him, squinting up at him as if he was a complete stranger.

"Hey," he greeted.

She looked different. Younger, more relaxed.

"Hi. I'm looking for a Dexter Scott." Her voice was very formal.

"You found him."

She pulled a very tattered page from *Western Horsemen* out of her back pocket and pointed to a small four-line classified ad. "This says he's looking for a good person to help with his horses. Must be willing to put in an honest day's work. Horse and cattle experience a plus. Is the position filled?"

"Might be," he said. He'd missed her eyes, the defiant tilt of her chin.

"Oh." She seemed deflated, but then continued. "I have my own horses and quite a bit of experience with cattle."

"I'm looking for someone with experience with wild cattle."

"I've got that. I've wrestled out the biggest monsters you can imagine."

"Oh, I can imagine."

"So what do you think?"

"I'd need to see your references."

She nodded. "I think that one of the ranchers I worked for might give me good references. He's sold his ranch and he's learning how to settle down in a retirement community in Arizona."

Dexter felt his heart expand.

Clem said, "I was looking for a cowboy that would take me on. Someone who has a lot of experience with horses and wild cows."

His heart throbbed. "I don't know. Why don't you ask him?"

"I'm still wondering about the job."

"It's still open for the right man."

"Man?"

"Person," he amended.

"You don't have any preconceived notions about women being as good as men?"

"None at all."

She looked around. "You pruned the rosebush."

He nodded. "And I fixed up the inside."

"Looks nice."

"It's waiting for me to carry a special lady over the threshold."

DEXTER WAS STANDING very close to her. She could feel him touch her with his eyes and knew that she'd made the right decision. It wasn't until she'd seen his ad in the magazine and read between the lines that he wanted her to come home to him. Clem had been happier than she'd been in a long time. But one piece of unfinished business had still niggled. She'd needed to know if she meant as much to a certain cowboy as he did to her.

"I love you, Clem."

The words hung in the bright desert morning.

"It's about time you told me that," she said.

"What?"

"I've been waiting since I was in the hospital for you to tell me that."

"Blame Randy."

"Randy?"

"Randy said that if I told you I loved you right away, you wouldn't follow your dream."

Clem was quiet. Randy had probably been right. And he'd probably known that after wandering around for a few months, she'd be ready to settle down, have a few kids to play on that grass Dexter said he was going to cultivate.

"You need to lock your gates," Clem replied instead. Her heart was hammering. "I drove right through them this morning. A man could get hurt leaving all his gates open."

"Only if he's scared."

"Are you scared?"

He shook his head. "Not me. I can do anything, survive anything. I can even cry."

Clem nodded, smiling into his dear face. It was a wonder that she'd lasted as long as she had. Three whole months without him. Ninety lonely days thinking about him, wondering if he loved her as much as she loved him.

"I needed to go away. Randy knew that. You knew that." Clem felt her throat tighten. "But I'm ready to come back and start a new life."

She could hear him suck his breath in. "A new life?"

"One with you."

He stared at her such a long time Clem thought maybe she was mistaken.

"Are you sure?" His voice was strained. "You can have as much time as you want. I'm not going anywhere."

"Oh, I'm sure. I think I love you, Dexter Scott."

"You only think?"

She laughed. "I know. I knew the moment I kissed you." Clem felt the joy of that knowledge spread through her body.

Dexter said quietly, "I knew when we rode back home after New Horse tossed me."

They smiled, both embarrassed.

"New Horse is great," she said awkwardly. "And I have more than one reference as to my skills. Will you take me on?"

Dexter considered her for such a long time, it was impossible for Clem to know what he was thinking. She could only see the love blazing at her from those moss-green eyes.

"Well, Scott?" she prompted, her voice husky. "What do you say about a partnership?"

Dexter pulled her into a tight hug. She could feel the accelerated thump of his heart. "Only if it's for life."

Clem squeezed her eyes shut to hold back the tears. She nodded, coming to an understanding that Joanna must have known all along. "Yes. Yes. It's all for life."